A PENNANT FOR
THE KREMLIN

by Paul Molloy

A PENNANT FOR THE KREMLIN

AND THEN THERE WERE EIGHT

A PENNANT FOR
THE KREMLIN

by PAUL MOLLOY

DOUBLEDAY & COMPANY, INC., GARDEN CITY, NEW YORK

1964

All of the characters in this book are fictitious, and any re-
semblance to actual persons, living or dead, is purely coin-
cidental.

Library of Congress Catalog Card Number 64–13864
Copyright © 1964 by Doubleday & Company, Inc.
All Rights Reserved
Printed in the United States of America
First Edition

To the star, Helen, and the supporting cast of *And Then There Were Eight*, Paul, Georgia, Shonagh, Nelda, Marcia, Lisa, Barbara, and Mark.

Armistead E. Childers stared angrily into the eyes of the President of the United States, a mere eight feet away. Rage brought a wetness to his fingers as they curled around the gold handle of the letter opener. Suddenly the eyes of the two men met and Childers could contain his fury no longer. With the fitful gait of agedness he stepped forward. "Fool!" he snarled. "This is the speech of a fool!" He moved closer, now, and his hand came up and he bent down and flicked the talking figure off the television set.

The outburst made the old man tired and he walked slowly back to his desk and returned the letter opener to its usual place. He sat down, wearily patted the bouffant wisps of handsome white hair back into place and stared at the opened newspaper before him. He read again, for the third time that morning, the account of the interview with the Secretary of State, bristling as he paused on the paragraph in which the Soviet Union was charged with "continued bad faith," on the disarmament issue. He had circled it with a red pencil and scrawled the word *abominable* alongside. Now he picked up the pencil and wrote *Warmonger!* and underlined it twice.

He pressed the buzzer beneath the edge of the desk and kept his finger on it until the door to his secretary's office opened and Miss Wiley minced in unsteadily. She was unsteady because she carried two cups of tea in her hands, two paper napkins under one arm, her dictation book under the other, and a ballpoint pen clutched horizontally between her teeth. During the twenty-two years she had worked for Childers, Adelaide Wiley had brought him a cup of black tea with lemon every morning at eleven o'clock, and had one with him; it had become a ritual, the day's sole intimacy between the two. Like her boss, Miss Wiley had never married and she was painfully aware of the whispers that circulated about the huge Childers office about her. There had once been a basis for the whispers, of course, because Miss Wiley entertained some daring hopes involving Childers and herself when she became his private secretary. Under the circumstances, what unmarried girl of thirty would have been without them? But that was twenty-two years ago, and the hopes had been dead a long, long time. Now there was only the daily cup of tea, sipped in silence.

Miss Wiley's feeling for Childers, especially over recent years, had been one of anxiety mingled with a frustrated, maternal-like desire to protect him. The man, for reasons she could not account for, had become obsessed with the idea that the United States government was knowingly headed for nuclear war with Russia. He was convinced that communism and capitalism were compatible, that the two systems should coexist peaceably. There was absolutely no reason, he felt, for a continual cold war which he cursed as the creation of the armament trust. He was plainly not a Communist; indeed, he considered himself a more patriotic citizen than most because of his keen awareness of the dangers of an endless stand-off between Washington and Moscow. Two years ago he had taken to writing letters to newspapers and magazines, pleading for the United States to "lead the way" with immediate nuclear disarmament. The Communists could be trusted to follow suit, he argued, because they wanted peace as much as Americans did—perhaps more. Because of his position in the business world —president of Childers Hotels of Distinction—his controversial stand drew a small following among some areas of the intellectual community, but it also attracted the inevitable coterie of crackpots and Communist sympathizers.

At the beginning, Childers was simply considered a harmless eccentric whose peculiar notions would likely have gone unnoticed were it not that he owned eighteen hotels. Then, while vacationing in Europe about a year ago, Childers had found himself in Vienna at the same time that the Russian premier was making a state visit to Austria. Somehow, through a maneuver that was never made clear, Childers was granted an audience with the Soviet leader—a meeting that had spawned an immediate friendship. It turned out that the premier had heard good things about "Comrade Childers," and he invited "this dedicated man of peace and friend of the Soviet Union" to spend a few days with him at his resort on the Caspian Sea. Childers did, and returned home more enthused than ever over the sincerity of his new friend. Suddenly he was in demand for lectures, but now his detractors saw him as a man with an evil doctrine, an avowed pro-Communist and quite possibly a traitor.

Adelaide Wiley knew he was none of these things, so her protective instinct had much to feed on.

A little timidly (despite her long tenure Miss Wiley had never felt completely at ease with Childers) she set the tea down in front of him, and some of it spilled into the saucer. "I'll clean it up," she said, removing the pencil from her mouth.

"Never mind that now," said Childers, an irritation in his voice. "Get Daniels and Morris in here. And who has my will—you or Daniels?"

"Your will?" said Miss Wiley. "I don't have it. It must be with the lawyers."

"Then tell Daniels to bring it in."

Miss Wiley used Childers' phone to call the company lawyers, whose offices were down the hall. Childers soaked the tea out of his saucer with the napkin and studied the gold-lettered legend around the rim, *"Childers Hotels of Distinction."* He was proud of the chain which his father had left him, an only child, when it consisted of only four hotels. Now there were eighteen and soon, when the resistance of Horizon Enterprises broke down, there would be twenty. An even twenty . . . this had long been his dream. Herman Bradley, his vice-president, was with the Horizon people in Chicago now, and it was only a matter of time before they sold.

Cup in hand, he walked to the window. A light rain had started to fall over Manhattan and for a moment he was amused by the quaint kaleidoscope of black umbrellas bobbing along Fifth Avenue, forty-two floors below. His gaze swept upward again, and directly in his line of vision rose the magnificent gray towers of the flagship hotel, the Childers-New York. It was a happy sight, and he wished he could be happy . . .

Leonard Daniels, the tall, red-haired senior attorney of the firm, took his usual seat at the far end of the leather couch and folded his arms, frowning; he carried a permanent frown. Tom Morris, a recent addition to the legal department, sat at the other end, crossed and uncrossed his legs, took out his pipe, changed his mind, returned it to his pocket and fiddled nervously with the large brown folder on his lap.

Childers returned to his desk and looked at the lawyers. "Anybody heard from Bradley?" he asked.

"Not today," Daniels said. "I talked with him Tuesday and it's still as I told you. Horizon's just about set to let the hotels go, but you won't get away with just the hotels. You're going to have to buy Horizon Enterprises kit and caboodle."

Childers grunted. "For those Chicago locations, it's worth it. Bradley's a good man; he knows what he's doing and he can dump the caboodle on somebody else later. I want those hotels. Now then, something more urgent. You have the will?"

Morris stood up quickly, plucking a sheaf of long white sheets from the folder.

"Tear it up," Childers said, before Morris reached his desk.

"Tear it up?" Morris said, looking first at Daniels then at Childers.

"Tear it up."

Morris sat down again. Slowly he tore the sheaf in half, then tore the halves in half again. He looked around the room, self-consciously, decided against the clumsy walk to the wastebasket and finally stuffed the clumps of paper in his coat pocket, the one that held the pipe. It made a bulge on his hip, and he felt embarrassed.

"Don't look so shocked," Childers scolded. "I have no kin to leave it to, anyway, so it's no disaster." Childers left his chair, walked the length of the office to the fireplace, and leaned on the mantelpiece. "I'm changing my will," he said, his chin jutting out.

Miss Wiley coughed gently and looked at her shoes. Morris went for his pipe again, and with it came a cluster of torn paper that fluttered to the floor; he desperately wished he were back in his own office.

Daniels said nothing; in fact, he wasn't especially curious because he had been through these impulses before. Once, Childers had changed his will to leave his entire fortune to the American Indians because "we white men stole them blind." A week or so later he had had second thoughts and the Indians were promptly disinherited. On another occasion, impressed by a tract on antivivisection, he had directed Daniels to add a codicil to the will giving one million dollars to the cause. Again, disenchantment set in and the clause was stricken out shortly thereafter.

Childers nodded to Miss Wiley and said, "Take this down." He walked to the window and looked into the rain for a full minute. Finally, still with his back to the others, he spoke slowly, deliberately:

"This is my last will and testament. I, Armistead Ernest Childers, president and sole owner of Childers Hotels of Distinction . . . being of sound mind . . . and in full possession of my faculties . . . do hereby revoke any and all other wills and testaments made by me except for provisions made earlier for my personal secretary of many years, Miss Adelaide Wiley, and do hereby bequest and—uh, devise . . . all my property, both real and personal . . . to the . . . to the government of the Soviet Union."

Childers turned from the window and walked back to the chair. Miss Wiley coughed again and became studiously engrossed in the shape and color of her pen. Morris's face blanched, and it looked as if he had sneezed into an ash tray; he stole a glance at Daniels who gave him a here-we-go-again look and stared at the ceiling.

Childers put his head in his hands, closed his eyes and continued: "I make this provision . . . realizing that it will be . . . it will be . . . criticized in some quarters . . . and that my . . . my patriotism will be questioned. Nevertheless, it is my hope that Ameri— that right-thinking people will see my decision as . . . prompted . . . by a sincere desire . . . for understanding between the United States and the Soviet Union . . . It is also my express wish that the government of the Soviet Union use all moneys accruing from this bequest . . . exclusively to . . . further the cause of world peace which we all cherish. That's all, Miss Wiley. Type it up right away."

When the door closed behind Miss Wiley, Childers asked Daniels, "Well, any comment?"

"Do you really want my comment?" Daniels said.

"Of course."

"Are you serious about all this?"

"Very serious."

"Well, my first thought is what in hell are the Russians going to do with eighteen American hotels and—"

Childers smiled. "Twenty hotels."

"—with twenty hotels, and my second thought is you're going to some extreme to make your point."

"Sometimes you have to take extreme measures, Daniels. Maybe this will shake up somebody in Washington."

"I think a lot of people are going to be shook up."

"Did you hear the President's speech last night? I got it on television this morning. My God, Daniels, he as much as called them liars and cutthroats! That's no way to reach an understanding. You don't go around calling the other fellow a cutthroat and a liar."

"I don't think the President was quite that forceful."

"Just about. We've got to learn to trust the people we're negotiating with. Without trust, nobody's going to get anywhere."

Daniels winced. "You trust them? All the way?"

"I know this man, Daniels. I lived with him for a week at his summer place last year, and we've been corresponding. That's all he can talk about—getting along together, us and them. But we charge him with bad faith and Washington keeps yapping that we've got the stuff to blow them off the earth. No wonder he's frustrated."

"Oh, he's frustrated all right," Daniels said wryly. He didn't feel up to another argument with Childers; the two had gone over the same ground innumerable times, and he felt they were both talked out. The whole boring business was academic, anyway, because in a few days Childers would change his mind about the will again. Daniels was glad that the copies of the original were still intact in his office.

Miss Wiley returned with the typewritten document and six copies; she placed the original on Childers' desk and gave the copies to Morris who was delighted with the chance to come to life. "Thank you ever so much," he gushed, putting the copies in his folder.

Miss Wiley gave Childers her pen and he signed his name slowly and in large, clear letters. "You two men will sign as witnesses," he said.

After they had signed, Childers got his hat from the clothes closet and said: "I'm going to the club for lunch, and then I'm going home for the day. Miss Wiley, have Martin bring the car up front." At the door, he paused and managed a light laugh, a little like a cackle. "I'd sure like to see their faces in Washington when they hear about this," he said. "This is a big day in my life."

It was indeed. While Martin, the chauffeur, was driving his boss to the club, Herman Bradley was in the Chicago penthouse office of Jack Huggins, sportsman, playboy, and majority stockholder of Horizon Enterprises, affixing his signature to quite another document—the bill of sale whereby Childers Hotels of Distinction acquired Horizon Enterprises.

Kit and caboodle.

When he telephoned New York with the news, Miss Wiley told him that Childers wouldn't be in until the next morning. "Why don't you call him on the car phone?" she said. "He's left the club by now and you can catch him on his way to Long Island. He's been terribly upset all morning, and this Chicago deal is just the thing to get him out of it."

It was nearing two-thirty and Martin had the limousine rolling gently down the slope that soon would lead into the driveway of the Childers estate, when the call was put through. Martin smiled, because the boss had dozed off again as he often did on the ride home. "The phone is ringing, sir," he said, turning down the radio. The phone rang again. "You have a call, Mr. Childers," he said, raising his voice.

But Childers was unable to take the call. He was dead.

And so it was that on that rainy July afternoon the Soviet Union came into possession of Childers Hotels of Distinction, and Horizon Enterprises—kit and caboodle.

The kit consisted of two luxurious hotels fronting Lake Michigan on Chicago's opulent North Side.

The caboodle included a small string of sporting goods stores, a swimming pool franchise that hadn't shown a profit in years, and a half interest in an automatic coffee vendor.

And the Chicago White Sox, currently tied for third place in the American League.

2

In all his years as probate judge, fleshy Archibald Dearing had never felt so important, nor had his small, somber courtroom contained such a cluster of celebrities. And seldom had it seemed as sultry—wall-to-wall humanity perspiring from the oppressive August heat and the baking lights of the television setup. Clumps of greenish-blue smoke floated about, like miniature icebergs nudged to and fro by fans that hissed at each other from across the room, and through the haze Judge Dearing stared at the chattering gaggle of baseball old-timers, syndicated columnists, and television technicians with stern, watery eyes.

He brought down his gavel with a solemn thwack. "I must remind you again," he intoned, "that this is a court of law, and not a circus. I will not proceed until we have order."

The babble abated somewhat, and although several newsmen continued to talk in low tones at the press table up front, Judge Dearing pretended not to hear them.

"In view of the heat and discomfort," he said, "I'd like to bring this hearing to a close as soon as possible." He looked about the room and added: "Is there anyone else who wishes to be heard?"

Before anyone could come forward he turned to Daniels, the corporation counsel now without a corporation: "Didn't you tell me, Mr. Daniels, that there is a representative of the Russian government here?"

Daniels, seated at a table before the bench and frowning, as usual, stood up. "Yes, your honor. As executor of the Childers estate, I went to Washington to confer with the Russian Ambassador, Mr. Leonid Galynin. I discussed the terms of the will with him, and he assigned the first secretary to the embassy, Mr. Stepan Bukharov, to attend this hearing."

"Of course," Judge Dearing said. "Mr. Bukharov, would you step forward?"

Bukharov, an immaculately dressed man, plump and black-haired, rose from his chair and peered at the judge through thick glasses. "I assume," Judge Dearing said, "that your ambassador has notified his government about this matter?"

"That is my understanding," Bukharov replied, standing stiffly erect.

"May I ask if the embassy has received any instructions from Moscow?"

"I am not in a position to say."

"You don't know?"

"I have not been informed."

"And you are here, I take it, simply to take note of the proceedings and report to your superiors in Washington?"

"I am here as an observer, at the invitation of Mr. Daniels."

"Thank you, Mr. Bukharov. That will be all."

Judge Dearing watched the wire service reporters lumber out toward telephones to report to their offices that the Russian official, who had been expected to make a crucial pronouncement, had said nothing. He felt a little sorry for them because they clearly had run themselves ragged since that mischievous—or was he more than mischievous?—old Childers had died.

The swift stroke that had gently cut Childers down in the back seat of his car had been a news natural for weeks. It was more than a story—it was a multiplying controversy. For a man to buy a Major League baseball team was news enough; for a man to buy a Major League baseball team and then promptly die was, at the very least, a phenomenal crisis. As one cynical sports writer had titillated his readers: "In the overcrowded record book of baseball there's always room for another first, and crotchety Armistead Childers came up with a beauty. He owned a Major League club for all of two hours, about the time it takes to wrap up nine innings. How do you top that?"

Childers himself, of course, had supplied the answer on publication of the will by putting the Kremlin in possession of the Chicago White Sox. This was no longer just a continuing headline; it was a many-sided furor.

There was, for instance, the moral angle. How could an American citizen turn against his country in such crude manner if he were in his right senses? "Mr. Childers," thundered one editorial, "leaped into his grave gleefully thumbing his nose at Uncle Sam."

There was the matter of legal technicalities. Was it permissible for an American citizen to leave his estate to a foreign government? There were some who said that a man could make whatever gift he chose to the British government or to the Italian government—why, then, could he not do likewise with the Russian government? But, the debate continued, the Communists were enemies of the United States! True, came the rejoinder, but the two countries were at peace (more or less), and not in a state of war. After four days of ponderously embarrassed silence, the Department of Justice finally delivered itself of an opinion: "In the United States a citizen may bequeath his estate to whomever he wishes, under normal conditions, and under circumstances not calculated to impose any hardship on this country or its people, collectively or as individuals. The U.S. government does not plan to interfere in this matter at this moment." The gobbledygook settled nothing.

There was also the plain business and finance approach. What would happen to those hotels? Would Russia run them? If not, would she sell them? Lease them? Turn them into consulate and trade offices, perhaps? And what would all this do to international relations which for years had been, at best, strained?

Lastly, but infinitely more controversial, there was the sports angle. When news of what had happened reached the baseball commissioner, Russell Kirk, he was too stunned for comment. There was no precedent for a thing like this and without a precedent to go on the burly, pink-faced opportunist was like an astronaut with claustrophobia; he was simply unable to function. He quickly went into seclusion, spent six hundred dollars on long-distance telephone calls, and emerged to announce with vigorous befuddlement that he would make no announcement until he had conferred with the president of the American League. Then, in a fuzzy clash of clichés, he asked everyone in baseball to refrain from comment "until the dust settles and everything blows over." His wish was met with bombastic diffidence by Bunny Beadle, the Sox's acrobatic second baseman and player representative on the team. "Kirk can go take a galloping jump," he said, tonguing his chewing tobacco to the other cheek. "Anybody thinks we're going to work for a bunch of Commies, they're crazy."

Horace Bratton, the soft-spoken, one-armed Bostonian who had managed the Sox for nine years, was more restrained. "I got just one thing on my mind," he said, boarding the team's chartered plane for Detroit, "a four-game series with the Tigers." Sadly, the players didn't share his serenity; the Tigers swept the series, toppling Chicago into fourth place.

In the days following Childers' death, newspapers and magazines reeled from an onslaught of angry, near-violent letters to the editor. Some indignant writers demanded that the U.S. government immediately seize Childers' properties. Others insisted that if Russia did acquire the estate, Washington should break off relations with Moscow. A few were so incensed they wanted Childers' body exhumed and shipped to Russia for reburial "where he belongs." (At the height of the indignation, one disturbed fan hurled himself from his ninth-story apartment window, leaving a note warning that Russian acquisition of the White Sox was the subtle prelude to the Communist invasion of America, leaving him no reason to live. But in an unnerving postscript the distraught soul obscured the import of his immolation by identifying himself as a stanch disciple of the lowly New York Mets.)

In time, however, a portion of the public feeling began to mellow. The opinions of cooler heads were heard across the land, questioning the wisdom of so much hullabaloo and urging an end to panic. Among dispassionate thinkers, it was obvious that Childers' will would be ruled invalid. Other stoics minimized the alarm with predictions that Moscow would tactfully decline the inheritance. And there were the incurable optimists who horned in on the dilemma with visions of turning the queasy predicament into a master stroke of diplomacy: Call Childers' bluff and play ball on his terms, they prodded, and prove again to the world, especially to the neutrals, that no crisis could suppress America's bold sense of humor. One weighty news magazine had come close to embracing that notion with this punchline to its report: "Roguish Armistead Childers fired the shot heard around the world of baseball, and heaven knows it needed it—right in the arm."

With this theory, whimsical as it was, the American League club owners seemed to be in accord: Two days before the probate hearing, they voted unanimously to award the Sox franchise to the designated heirs, "at least until the end of the current season."

Judge Dearing, who had greeted that decision with considerable relief, now looked about the room again and said: "I'm told there is someone here from the Department of Justice."

A slender young man with a crewcut stood amid the center seats. "Your honor," he called out, "my name is Joel Rhodes and I'm from the Department of Justice. The department merely wished to be present for the record since these proceedings involve the transfer of American property to a foreign government."

Just for a moment, Judge Dearing resented the implacable eyes of the camera lenses. His trousers were sticking to him most uncomfortably, and he felt a nagging urge to pluck them off his shanks. But he suffered silently and said: "If that is all, then, I'm prepared to rule on the—"

At these words a cadaverous, balding man who had been talking to Kirk loped forward. "If it please the court," he said, tripping over a mound of television cables, "I am Lionel Harris, counsel for the baseball commission. I represent Mr. Kirk."

"Yes?" said Judge Dearing, squirming covertly on the muggy leather.

"I request the court's permission to question Mr. Daniels. We would like to know more of what transpired between Mr. Daniels and the Russian Ambassador in Washington."

"Are you suggesting that Mr. Daniels is withholding information?"

"Not precisely, your honor. But Mr. Daniels is executor of the Childers estate, and it appears to us that he has made precious little known to this court as to the status of the ball club."

"Are you entering a contestation of the will?"

"No, we are not—that is, not officially. But I need not remind this court that a great deal is at stake here; not just the fate of a baseball club, but perhaps the fate of the entire profession."

"I'm not quite clear—" Judge Dearing began.

Daniels came to his feet. "Your honor, perhaps I can help matters along. Evidently Mr. Harris feels that I haven't advised the court fully on conversations between Ambassador Galynin and myself. To get to the heart of the matter, I think he and the commission want to know what the reaction of the Soviet government has been. I should like to remind Mr. Harris that I am not bound to comply with his request since the commission is merely an interested party, and not an heir."

"I know that," Harris said, "but—"

"Still," Daniels interrupted, "I can appreciate the very real interest that the commission would have in the matter. And I will tell Mr. Harris that I don't have the slightest inkling of the Soviet government's attitude at this point."

"You've already told us, haven't you," Judge Dearing said, "that there has been no statement from the Russian government?"

"That's right," Daniels said. "Not to me, anyway. I have been in close touch with both Mr. Galynin and Mr. Bukharov, here, and I've been assured that no directive has come from their government. I assume they're maintaining an official silence until the will has been probated. It may be they anticipated some trouble. It wouldn't surprise me if they were just as mixed up over this whole mess as we are."

Harris wasn't satisfied. "I must say you seem to take this matter lightly," he said, glaring at Daniels. "This is a most unusual situation. Here we have a beloved baseball club about to fall in the hands of the Communists. Do you realize the seriousness of all this? Does the court realize it?"

"Mr. Harris," said Judge Dearing coldly, "the court realizes that all matters involving wills are serious. The court also realizes that it's time you came to the point."

Harris looked over his shoulder at Kirk, leaning against the wall at the rear of the courtroom, took a deep breath and said: "If I may say so, your honor, the commission is not convinced that Mr. Childers was entirely responsible when he—"

"I object!" Daniels shouted.

"Mr. Harris," the judge said, leaning over, "you have just made, or were about to make, a serious charge—a charge that is tantamount to challenging the will. I ask you again: Are you contesting it?"

"We are not."

"Good! Then I might suggest, since the matter has come

up, that the commission is hardly in a position to do so. The commission does not own the Chicago White Sox or any other ball club. The team was the property of Mr. Childers and in this country, Mr. Harris, a man may give his fortune to whomever he wishes. There is no law that says Mr. Childers can't leave his estate to the Russian government. You may call it an unwise decision, but it is not illegal. And I have no grounds on which to reverse it."

"But, your honor," Harris exclaimed, "baseball is our national pastime! It belongs to the public, and the White Sox belong to the people of Chicago!"

"It's a little hot for idealistic nonsense, Mr. Harris. Baseball may be a national pastime, but it's also a business enterprise operated for profit. Or haven't you noticed that there are turnstiles at every park? As to ownership, I'll say this: Until recently, the Chicago White Sox belonged to Mr. Jack Huggins of Horizon Enterprises, who sold it to Mr. Childers, who gave it to the Russian government."

In spite of the whirring fans, the room seemed to be in absolute silence. Judge Dearing leaned back, stretching his humid legs, and the two television dollies bore down on him like a pair of small cannons. "It is the judgment of this court," he said, "that the will of Mr. Armistead Ernest Childers be admitted to probate. This court is now adjourned."

As Daniels, Harris, and the other principals collected their papers, Bukharov remained in his chair, scribbling furiously into a small notebook.

3

Leonid Galynin removed his pince-nez, smiled and gently rubbed the small, pink welts on each side of his nose. Daniels, who had believed pince-nez to be extinct, was mildly fascinated by what he took as a gesture of affection, but he wished Galynin would stop rubbing and come to the point. He had been in the Russian Ambassador's office almost ten minutes and Galynin hadn't even mentioned Childers' name so far; he had talked of little except a vacation he was starting at the end of the month.

"August," he rambled on, "it is a good month to go from Washington. You agree?"

"Yes, it can get terribly hot around here," Daniels said, wondering if his impatience was beginning to show.

Galynin smiled again and leaned back on the swivel chair with half-closed eyes, as if Daniels' remark called for deep reflection. Daniels studied him, impressed by the difference between Galynin and his first secretary, Bukharov, who sat sullenly beside his superior's desk, hands on knees and his eyes blank as agates behind the thick glasses.

In contrast with the pudgy, churlish Bukharov, Galynin was tall and heavy with very little fat. He reminded Daniels of a wrestler—not the flabby, fraud-type on television—and the abundance of pockmarks on his face would have given him an added air of toughness if it weren't that he smiled so much (Daniels wondered about that smile) and wore a pince-nez. Finally he abandoned his reverie.

"Now we discuss the purpose of your visit," he said. "It has taken much time but my government was waiting for the decision of your courts. You will understand."

"I understand," Daniels said.

"Also, your courtesy in coming to Washington again. I thank you."

"Not at all."

"I must tell you, Mr. Daniels—since I am here, never have I seen so much excitement."

"It's been a blockbuster all right," Daniels said, wistfully eying the papers on Galynin's desk.

"A what?"

"It's caused a lot of fuss, a real commotion."

"Yes. You Americans are very—how do you say?—spirited on things that concern us."

"Hysterical," Bukharov broke in, tapping his fingers on his knees.

"Mr. Ambassador," Daniels said, "you must remember this has been an unusual event."

"Ah, but you are so emotional! The Cuban incident, what your people called the crisis . . . This"—he slapped the papers in front of him—"has been more trouble!"

"Really? Well, curiosity is a human trait." Now Daniels felt he had to wheedle the ambassador. "I must say I'm rather curious myself," he chuckled.

Galynin took the hint. "As I told you on the telephone, I have received a first report from my government on the matter of the will of Mr. Childers. It is my duty to communicate this to you so that you may take the action necessary."

Daniels relaxed and found a cigarette; this was it. Bukharov stopped his finger-tapping.

"First," Galynin went on, "I must pass to you the appreciation of my government for the good gesture of Mr. Childers. It was a nice kindness by him."

"It certainly was." Daniels was embarrassed and he could think of nothing else to say.

"But I am instructed to tell you that, in general, my government does not wish to take a selfish advantage of the generosity of Mr. Childers."

He consulted his papers and continued: "I will list to you the recommendations. First, in the matter of the legacy of money: There is a large sum, and it is the request of the Soviet government that this money immediately is placed into the international disaster fund for the victims of the earthquake in Bolivia last month. The Soviet government is of the opinion that this will meet with the wishes of Mr. Childers, that it will make known his love for people, his wanting for international friendship. The distribution of this money will be arranged by our delegation to the United Nations."

"Yes," said Daniels, who now was making notes.

"If you wish not to make notes now, I shall see that a complete report is prepared for you on this matter."

"Thank you, Mr. Ambassador."

"Second, in the matter of the company of Childers Hotels of Distinction: This company consists of eighteen hotels in the northeastern United States, and in Florida, and in Georgia and in Texas. Mr. Childers was a true citizen of the world and a beloved friend of the Soviet Union, and my government wishes to conform with the spirit of his kind deed. My government does not think it will be practical to enter into the operation, you understand, of the hotels. My government feels that they belong to the workers of Mr. Childers who did so much to bring success to him. So it is our wish that these properties become owned by the workers who deserve the fruits of their labor. It is the hope of the Soviet government that the transfer of ownership by the workers of Mr. Childers is arranged very soon. This will be arranged by a committee of you, Mr. Daniels; Mr. Bradley, the vice-president of Childers Hotels of Distinction; Mr.

Bukharov, and Mr. Valentin Kononov, our trade attaché here at the embassy."

Daniels nodded noncommittally and Galynin, riffling through his papers, gave Bukharov a half-nod. "Mr. Bukharov has made the suggestion that the name of the company should be changed to People's Hotels of Distinction. But it is felt by myself, and others, that it is good not to do this so that all can remember the heroic name of Mr. Childers, and the workers can show the signs on the hotels to the children and talk of the benefactor who was a friend of all the world."

Daniels visualized a sign on Park Avenue reading, THE PEOPLE'S-NEW YORK HOTEL, and shuddered. "I think that keeping the Childers name is good thinking on your part," he said.

"Three," Galynin said. "We come to the matter of the legacy of the other company of Mr. Childers, the Horizon Enterprises: in this company there are two hotels, located in the city of Chicago, Illinois. It is the request of the Soviet government that these hotels also become the property of the workers of Mr. Childers, in the manner of the other hotels.

"The Horizon Enterprises also is the owner of five establishments that sell equipment for the athletics. My government directs that these establishments will be sold and that one third of the money is placed in the disaster fund of the earthquake in South America. The two-thirds left of the money will be placed for the maintenance of the Soviet delegation to the United Nations. In the matter of the smaller company of the Horizon Enterprises that constructs tanks for the swimming amusement, this also will be sold and the money will be used in the maintenance of our delegation to the United Nations. Also the interest—I believe it is a half-interest—in the company that makes coffee into the machines."

Galynin poured himself a glass of water and offered some to Daniels, who declined. Galynin emptied the glass slowly, replaced the pince-nez atop his nose and swung his chair to face Daniels.

"Now we are at the matter of the other property, the club of baseball that is called the Chicago White Sox. The Soviet government believes that this is a very special matter. It feels that during the last years much good friendship has been made between the Soviet Union and the United States under the—shall we say—under the banner of sports and of culture, especially in the culture exchange that has existed for a little time. We have been happy, you and us, with the international friendship that was made between the two countries in the glorious Olympics. We wish to keep with the ideals of international friendship which were in the mind of Mr. Childers. For that reason, my government takes possession of the club of baseball."

"It does?" Daniels said, burning himself with his cigarette. He wished he hadn't put such a silly question.

"It is our feeling," Galynin said, "that much can be accomplished if we conduct the sport of baseball with auspices that will be mutual, in following the desires of Mr. Childers."

Daniels' frown became a crooked furrow. "I must say I'm a little astounded," he said. "Won't it be somewhat difficult to operate the club—I mean, under the circumstances?"

Galynin was not smiling now. "I am not able to inform you," he said, a little severely. "The answers will come from Mr. Mikhail Deborin who has been appointed by my government to be the leader of the White—uh, what is it?—ah, yes, the White Sox. By the way, Mr. Daniels, what does Sox mean?"

"It's a slang spelling for socks. It means stockings."

"What a strange name for an athletic organization. Why is it called that?"

"I don't know," Daniels said, feeling ill at the thought of People's Sox. "This Mr. Deborin—what does he do in Russia?"

"Mr. Deborin is the deputy chairman of the Central Council of the All-Union Committee on Sports and Culture."

"I see. Then he'd be the top man in sports in your country?"

"He is one of the high officials in athletics not only in the Soviet, but in the Union of Soviet Socialist Republics."

"That's very interesting. But does he know anything about baseball?"

"I am unable to tell you. I do not know him. This will have to wait until he arrives to this country."

"By the way, when does he get here?"

Bukharov sucked in his breath, as if the conversation bored him. "The embassy received a cablegram this morning," he said. "Mr. Deborin will arrive Saturday."

Daniels smiled wanly. "Well, this whole thing has taken quite a turn. If your man's going to be here in a couple of days, I'm going to have to get in touch with Bratton right away."

Galynin poured himself more water. "Bratton?"

"Horace Bratton, the White Sox manager. He's in charge of the team and—"

"Mr. Deborin is in charge," Bukharov interrupted tersely.

"Of course," Daniels said. "But the two of them are going to have to get together as quickly as possible. As soon as Mr. Deborin is settled, I suggest you have him contact Bratton, wherever the team is over the weekend, and—"

Bukharov interrupted again. "Mr. Daniels," he said, contempt now creeping into his voice, "one does not tell Mr. Deborin to go here or to go there, as one would speak to a common messenger. It will be your Mr. Bratton's task to make himself available to Mr. Deborin—at the convenience of Mr. Deborin."

"Of course," Daniels said, a little vexed.

"I should explain," Galynin said, "how important this matter is regarded by my government. As a deputy chairman in the Central Council, Mr. Deborin has a status equivalent to the rank of cabinet minister."

"I'm glad to hear that," Daniels said, recovering his composure, "but if you don't mind my going back to this again, I dearly hope he knows something about baseball."

Now it was Galynin's turn to be irritated. "Mr. Daniels, you seem to think, like many Americans, that the peoples of the Soviet Union are backward in many things. I wish you to know that it is the contrary. Our peoples not only are advanced in many things, but they also have been for many glorious years the—how do you say it?—the pioneers. As for an example, we are always amused when we read that it is the Americans who have invented the airplane, that it is the Americans who have invented the television. It is the contrary. The first principles of the airplane and the television were developed, very long ago, by scientists of the Soviet Union."

Daniels occupied himself with another cigarette and said nothing.

"I suppose," Galynin pursued, "you believe that the sport of baseball is an invention of you Americans?"

Daniels laughed. "Yes, I do."

"It is not."

"It isn't?"

"No. Have you ever heard of lapta?"

"Never. What does it mean?"

"Lapta is the father of your baseball. It is an ancient folk sport that originated in Russia a very long time ago, and it become the foundation of your sport of baseball."

"That's a new one on me. Why have we never heard of it?"

"Because we have not made a capitalist business, as you Americans do, of our athletics. But millions of people play lapta in Russia in the warm seasons."

"Is it much like our game?"

"Basically, yes. It is played by two groups—two teams of ten members on a square field that is seventy meters long. All players are on the field at all times, and they use a small ball that is made of cloth. Sometimes, they use a ball made of very soft rubber. A member of one group throws the ball to a member of the other group who must hit it with a round willow stick that is eighty centimeters long. This stick is the lapta."

"I see. What happens when your lapta man—we call him the batter—hits the ball?"

"The member who hits the ball, the batter, must run to the position of the man who has thrown it, and then to his own position before an opposing member strikes his body with the ball."

"You mean, to get him out somebody has to hit him with the ball? Doesn't that hurt?"

"The ball is soft. But it is more interesting than that. While the ball is in flight, the colleagues of the man who has thrown it must run about, trying to touch opposing members. As will be realized, the opposing members run away from them. The touching of an opponent while the ball is in motion is rewarded by one point."

"When do they change sides? When does the other team come up to bat—I mean up to lapta?"

"Ah, this is the great thrill of all. The ideal thing is for a member to catch the ball in flight and then to touch an opposing member. When this takes place, his organization then has its turn with the lapta."

Daniels rose to leave. "Tell me, Mr. Ambassador, have you ever seen a game of American baseball?"

"No, but I look forward to seeing some now."

"Well, I'm afraid you'll find our baseball and your lapta a little different."

"In the American way, do you try to hit the—uh, the batter with the ball?"

"Not as a rule. It happens, sometimes. When it does, the batter gets a walk to the base."

"They walk," Galynin mused. "How strange. Our lapta is more exciting because it is a test of endurance, so there is no walking. It is run, run, run all the time."

It was that kind of elegant summer morning when a man resented having to exhale, with a silky breeze making sensuous passes at the neck and a playful sun that brought blissful sneezes when one looked into its eye. But Mike Dewar felt only a pot-bellied uneasiness, as if his breakfast had snapped, crackled, and turned to stone. The jet bearing Mikhail Deborin was in its whining, downward soar, and he didn't like the looks of the reception committee.

As traveling secretary (and publicity director) for the White Sox for thirteen years, paunchy, wise-cracking Mike Dewar considered himself an authority on welcoming committees. The trouble with this one, he fretted, was that it was broken up into too many subcommittees—most of them uninvited—messing up the airport apron.

There was, for instance, the group of pickets parading up and down the esplanade in front of the terminal. It consisted of about twenty men and women (some with babies hurling bawls at the cloudless sky) with crudely crayoned placards that read *RUSSKY GO HOME* and *WATCH THE COMMIE DOUBLE-PLAY* and *FOUL BALL KIRK STRIKES OUT*—the last a discordant echo of the commissioner's timidity. This assortment glared at the Kirk group.

Kirk's group included Arnold Lang, president of the American League; his National League counterpart, Vernon Crowley, and a handful of lesser officials Dewar knew only through fleeting handshake. They stood almost shoulder to shoulder, and they glared, too. They glared at the police unit which, they felt, should be doing something about that rabble on the picket line.

The police group spent most of its time glaring at the press corps of reporters, photographers, and newsreel men who were hooting orders to stay behind the barricade until the plane taxied in. Unhappy about the restriction, this band, in turn, glared at Dewar's party which was limited to Beadle and "Gentleman Jim" Reeves, Sox captain and the league's most courteous pitcher. (Whenever one of his throws dusted a batter off the plate, Reeves would lope off the mound and apologize—a habit which umpires suspected he used to rest his arm). Reeves, on a four-day layoff between pitching assignments, was on hand to represent Bratton.

Dewar was worried because Beadle not only was glaring defiantly at the Russian group he was taunting its members with loud remarks that reflected on their lineage. Twice, already, Reeves had asked Beadle to hold his tongue, and Dewar hoped that some of Reeves' good manners would rub off on the scrappy second baseman. The Russian group, which was composed of Galynin, Bukharov, and their country's chief delegate to the United Nations, Leon Sobolev, seemingly didn't hear Beadle's observations. They were too busy glaring at all the other groups.

There was also an unofficial welcoming committee of curious hangers-on and airport personnel who had gotten wind that a big celebrity was about to land.

Like a large blue sliver peeling off the plane's breast, the passenger door opened and a stewardess stepped out, blinking, and stood to the side of the loading ramp, at the top. "I wonder what he looks like," Reeves said, as the first of the passengers followed.

"Look for a guy in a big fur cap," Beadle said, struggling with a bag of salted peanuts.

"Oh, sure," Dewar scoffed, "in this weather he'll be wearing a big fur cap, and maybe a pair of Siberian mukluks."

"Keep your eye on the Reds," Beadle said, "they'll spot him for us."

Sure enough, before Beadle had finished speaking, Galynin pointed excitedly at the emerging figure of a stocky, hawk-nosed man wearing a striped blue suit with large lapels, a black shirt and a black tie. The man did not see his compatriots waving at him; he had turned to assist a laughing young woman with intensely black hair who put her arm in his.

Dewar whistled softly. "We're not getting no Casey

Stengel," he whispered, "but any guy can pick himself a doll like that for a wife can't be all bad."

"He's got to be twice her age," Reeves said, noting the man's shaggy, silvery hair, some of it falling over his brow.

"Old enough to be her father," Beadle said out of the side of his mouth. "But look at that shirt and tie! This guy's been seeing too many gangster movies."

Suddenly there was a commotion as several reporters skirted the barricade and half-ran to the ramp. Galynin and his two companions fell into a jog, too, reaching the foot of the stairs at the same time. Confused by the melee, Deborin, with a wide smile that showed excellent teeth, threw himself on a lanky, sad-eyed man in a green blazer, and wrapped him in a bear hug. Unfortunately he was shouting his effusive *spasibos* (thanks) to an unnerved representative of the Kansas City *Star* who lost his pencil, his notebook, and two buttons off his blazer in the crush.

Now the placard carriers began a chant, "Russky Go Home!" that mounted in intensity as Dewar, Beadle, and Reeves found themselves pushed into the center of human swirl by dozens of the hangers-on who had come crashing through the gate. Above the din and the rhythmic chants from the picket line, Galynin was shouting in Russian but Deborin, now trying to look after the young woman, could not hear him. Finally, Bukharov stretched out an arm to grasp Deborin's attention and in so doing his hand slapped flush into the mouthful of peanuts belonging to Beadle who, as it happened, was trying to propel Dewar toward the bewildered deputy chairman.

"Who you pushing, you card-carrying jerk!" Beadle yelped, throwing an untalented punch that missed by a yard and came to a sickening stop in the vicinity of Commissioner Kirk's navel. Bukharov wrapped his arms around Beadle's waist and the two wrestled almost to their knees before a policeman managed to break them apart. As he was pulling himself together, Beadle saw the white flash almost upon him and twitched his head just enough for the egg to miss. It splattered, in a magnificent orangey eruption, on the front of Bukharov's neck and oozed gently down his clothes.

Another squished on his sleeve and now eggs—the rebels had come well armed—were swishing through the air and the scene looked like nothing so much as a snowball fight in a schoolyard, with artistic splats scoring in all directions. At least a dozen passengers scurried back into the plane.

In the pandemonium, Dewar managed to confront Deborin long enough to identify himself as traveling secretary. It didn't seem appropriate just then to go into his welcoming speech. Besides, he didn't get the chance; Deborin begged him to liberate the terrified woman on his arm and Dewar bullied his way through the mob to Sobolev's limousine, idling near the esplanade. Alertly, the chauffeur had opened all four doors and Dewar and his charge scampered in. Behind them stumbled Deborin, followed by Galynin; patting his crushed hat back into shape, Sobolev brought up the rear.

After the police had shooed everyone off the apron, Bukharov turned on Beadle. "See what you have done," he said, with a hiss in his voice. "They have gone without me!"

Beadle almost spat out the words. "Get yourself a cab, Commie!"

"And look at my suit," Bukharov said with a wry face. "The eggs, they have ruined it!"

"We'll pick up your man's luggage and take you where you're going," Reeves offered.

"I will not travel with you," Bukharov shouted. "I shall walk, first!"

Mustering as much dignity as was possible with egg yolk running down his trousers, Bukharov walked only as far as the taxi stand. But none of the drivers would take him because of what the unsightly dripping would do to their upholstery. Disconsolate, he walked back to Reeves and accepted his offer of a ride; Reeves put him in the front seat and told Beadle to sit in the back.

In the haughty Russian limousine, Sobolev was mortified to discover that Bukharov had been left behind in the
confusion. The Russians spoke among themselves in their
own language for a few minutes and Dewar, ignored, felt
about as cozy as a cricket in a birdhouse. He cupped a hand
on his chin and gazed idly at the passing countryside, wondering why the two words *belye chulki* kept coming up in
everybody's conversation. Probably a cuss word, he thought.
No, that couldn't be it; they wouldn't be swearing so much
in the presence of a lady though, Lord knew, they had
plenty to swear about. At last Deborin turned to him and
said:

"I am honored very much, Mr. Dewar, that at the airport
a man of such high post is meeting me."

"A pleasure," Dewar replied, exalted. He hoped he wasn't
blushing, for even his own people had never paid him such
a fine compliment.

"I did not expected," Deborin continued, "a representative of the United States government."

"What's that again?" Dewar said.

"I beg the pardon?" Deborin rejoined.

"I was begging yours. What was that bit about the government?"

"You are in the cabinet, are you not?"

Dewar wondered if he should laugh; foreigners had such
a queer sense of humor. "Not me," he said, searching for a
clue in Deborin's face.

"But you told me you were the Secretary of Travel."

"No, no, no! I'm the traveling secretary—for the club!"

Deborin reflected on that for about half a mile. "I was
not sure about this," he said, "because I do not know such
a post in your government." After another silence he said,
"But I thank you for your help at my daughter."

"Your daughter?"

"My daughter, Tasia."

This sounded like an introduction, so Dewar squirmed
into a half-turn and faced Tasia who sat between him and

Deborin, but before he could say anything she fixed him with the most extraordinary eyes Dewar had ever seen, and said, "You were very kind."

"That's all right," Dewar said, and suddenly he felt his shoelaces were too tight. "I don't want to sound like a wise guy but—your eyes, aren't they purple?"

Tasia's smile in the center of a face that had not a trace of make-up totally banished the airport incident from Dewar's mind. "Many people ask," she said. "They are a form of purple—lavender."

"Lavender? I've never heard of lavender eyes in this country!"

"It is rare in Russia, also. My mother had eyes of lavender."

The others resumed their animated conversation and as they talked Dewar learned from Tasia that she was twenty-two, an only child, and that her mother had died five years before. Since then she went almost everywhere with her father, acting as his companion-secretary. Dewar was surprised that she spoke English so well, and told her so.

"In Russia, it is an obligation in school," she said. "After my mother died my father decided he wanted to learn English, so I taught him."

"I wish I could handle your language," he said. "I keep wondering what that *belye chulki* means. That's all I keep hearing."

Tasia threw back her head and laughed again. "You will hear it often," she said. "It means white stockings."

The car turned onto Park Avenue and headed north toward 68th Street and the residence of the UN delegation, and Deborin turned his attention to Dewar again. He instructed him to return to Sobolev's apartments that evening, and to bring Bratton with him for a first conference.

Dewar said he would, and explained Bratton's absence at the airport—an afternoon game with the New York Yankees and a double-header the next day. Deborin was shocked to learn that the teams played just about every day and twice on Sundays. "They should have engagements one time in the week," he said, "so the people will not spend so much time away from their labors. There will be some changes."

Dewar was aching to learn what Deborin knew about baseball, but he didn't have the nerve to throw out a blunt question. He went to great pains to explain the current team standings and the prospects of the White Sox (six games behind the league-leading Yankees, their prospects were good), but Deborin—either by question or comment— gave no clue whatever. Suddenly he startled Dewar by mentioning Nelson's name.

"Your Jim Nelson," he said, "he is the one who guards the position of the outside, yes?"

"He's our third baseman," Dewar said.

"He is much talented, he stops all the balls, yes?"

"Best third baseman in the league," Dewar said, blinking at Deborin's knowledge.

"That is good. And this Ken—this Ken Power, he strikes the ball with much excellence?"

"It's Powers, not Power, and does he ever! Fabulous hitter."

"That is good, too. Last year he was decorated, that is so?"

"That's right. He got the Most Valuable Player award. Say, how come you know all this about those guys?"

Deborin plunged his long, hairy hand into his pocket and disengaged a small package of cards. Dewar saw, with nerve-wrenching dismay, that they were bubble-gum base-ball cards.

"Tasia found this," he said with a twinkle of pride. "Our airplane stopped at—what is the place?—Gander. Tasia, she enjoys sweets and she saw the American gum in the shop where we wait. It is foolish, this gum, but Tasia, she is curious. I tell her try it and she found a card. I was very surprised, you see, and I buy more. There is much information on the cards; this is very interesting."

Dewar wanted to sink into the seat. "It's a kid thing," he mumbled. "Children collect them."

"You will get some more for me." Deborin said.

"More cards?"

"Yes. It is good that we study the talents of the ball athletes who oppose us."

"But Mr. Deborin! You won't need that junk to—"

"You will get other cards. All of them. Tomorrow!"

"I'll do the best I can," Dewar said. Then he leaned back and once again stared out the window. This is a hell of a way, he thought, to run a railroad. And he wondered, too, what he would do with all that gum.

4

People often told Bratton they wondered why he didn't have an ulcer. The wonderment came from regular visitors to Comiskey Park in Chicago. Watching the destinies of the unpredictable White Sox, so adroit at squeaking through one-run victories and blowing five-run leads, was often an ulcerous hazard, and the afflicted marveled at Bratton's composure under duress. Bratton loved to tip his ever-present dark glasses to the top of his head and explain that he once had an ulcer, but it was located in his left arm. And he had left that arm near Mount Cassino long ago.

His philosophy was that he had enough things on his mind without cluttering it up with worry.

But the thing on his mind this moist Sunday afternoon in Yankee Stadium was responsible for the fresh teeth marks on the temples of his glasses. He wasn't worried—yet—but he was in meditation. Not about the Yankees winning the first game of the double-header; not about the off-and-on rain that had already delayed the second game twice; not even about Mrs. Bratton who got lonely when he went on the road and shortened the waiting with long afternoons in the movie houses, trying to overcome her depression.

He was concerned with last night's first encounter with Mikhail Deborin. The Russian had been businesslike and gentlemanly (though he could understand why Beadle had swung at Bukharov), but to learn that he was no longer team manager was upsetting. At least, it didn't look as if he would remain in charge. What Deborin had said was that he would take over as chairman of the club, and Bratton would become its deputy chairman. As far as Bratton was concerned, the title was almost obscene, and in the locker room he had warned the players—a man can't be placid all the time—that the first one to call him deputy chairman would be fined a hundred dollars.

Aware that Deborin didn't know the first catechism of baseball, Bratton was fairly sure he would at least be calling the shots on the field. But a fact was a fact: after nine years as boss, he was now a second banana.

With the fifth inning out of the way, Bratton was surprised to see Deborin, buttoned up to the neck in a raincoat, walk into the dugout. But the shocker was to see Bukharov follow him in.

Frequently during the first game the mammoth crowd had kept up a clamorous, hand-clapping we-want-Deborin cry in the stands. The fans were curious to see the foreigner sent from Moscow to manage the colorful Sox. Eventually they assumed he was not yet ready (or he was afraid) to make his public debut, and the din had subsided. Now Bratton hoped his visitors would stay inside the dugout and not venture onto the field.

"We have some points?" Deborin asked, looking about for a seat on the bench.

The Sox had just been retired in order. "No," Bratton said, "it's nothing to nothing."

"That is good," said Bukharov, motioning to the batboy to give him his seat. "Then nothing has happened that we should have seen." Several players looked at each other in mute disbelief. "I wouldn't say that," Bratton said. "We lost the first game."

"I was all afternoon in your museum," Deborin explained. "It is very beautiful, all those paintings. Tasia, she is still there."

"That's nice," Bratton said, irked at the Yankees' first run on a walk and two successive hits. "They've just gone ahead."

"We must equal our opponents," said Deborin, noticing a new stampede of clouds. "But it is sad that the clubs engage themselves in such a climate."

"There are seventy-five thousand people out there," Bratton said, "and a little rain doesn't bother them."

The Sox came to bat at the top of the seventh and Bratton was seized with a small elation when Beadle led off the inning with a walk. It soon subsided, however, for the next man struck out and the third was retired on an infield popout. Adding to the gloom was Deborin's poorly timed curiosity about the club's financial condition. He kept distracting Bratton with questions about player salaries, pay increases and bonuses (which he called production incentives). Suddenly, while Deborin was asking about travel expenses, Bukharov grabbed his arm and whispered hurriedly in his ear.

Deborin glared at home plate. "That man!" he shouted. "Call him back!"

"Who?" Bratton asked.

"That man with the stick!" Deborin said, pointing excitedly to the batter. "At once call him to me!"

Bratton bounded up the dugout steps, called time out and motioned to Salvatore Castinez, his shortstop who was digging in at the plate. Castinez, a Puerto Rican in his second year with the Sox, shrugged his massive shoulders and walked slowly back to the dugout.

"This is Sal Castinez," Bratton said. "He's one of my good hitters. What's the big idea?"

"What did you do?" Deborin asked, his nostrils a-quiver.

Castinez tapped a chunk of mud off his cleats. "Who? Me?"

"You!"

"When?"

"When you go to your position. What did you do?"

"I didn't do nothin'," Castinez said nonchalantly. "What d'you mean?"

"You did like this," Deborin yelled, his hand flying to his head and then to his chest.

"Oh, that," Bratton laughed. "He was making the sign of the cross."

"Aha!" Bukharov said in Deborin's ear, but this time out loud. "The sign of the cross. As I told you!"

"This will stop," Deborin said. "You will not do that. Never!"

"Just a minute," Bratton said. "What's wrong with his making the sign of the cross?"

"I forbid. No more."

"Oh, come on, now. It's something he likes to do when he comes up to bat."

Deborin fixed Bratton in his dark glasses. "Tell me, my friend, what does it mean?"

Bratton stuck his hand in his back pocket, and thought for a moment. "Well, to be honest, it doesn't mean a damn thing if he can't hit."

"Of course," Bukharov said, lurking behind Deborin.

The plate umpire, holding a soggy protector away from his chest, marched up to the dugout as the rhythmic hand-clapping started up again. "What's going on here?" he demanded. "Get a batter up there, and make it fast!"

Bratton patted Castinez on the rump and nodded toward the plate.

"Do not forget," Deborin said as Castinez left, "no cross." He turned to Bratton. "This is a place for the contest of athletes," he said. "This is not a church place. I am not permitting such things when I am chairman of the club."

Bratton idly wondered what Deborin would say if he learned that the Yankee land they were standing on, all six acres of it, was owned by the Knights of Columbus. "I can't see that it hurts anything," he said.

Ignominiously, Castinez struck out.

Deborin spoke almost with relish. "I do not see that it is helping," he said.

"Christian superstition," Bukharov muttered, getting back to his seat.

The Yankees held onto their one-run lead until the top of the ninth when the Sox put a man on first. Beadle flied out, and again it was Castinez's turn at bat. This time he made no outward gesture as he reached the plate but, unnoticed, he traced a tiny cross in the wet sand with the end of his bat. On the first pitch, his huge shoulders seemed to shudder as the bat swung on a low, inside throw and the ball soared in a mighty arc and struck below the lip of the left-field fence, three hundred and ten feet away.

Deborin was on his feet. "You see!" he shouted, as the base-runner galloped home from first. "You see what he does without your stupid sign of the cross!"

Castinez, a grin cracking his somber mulatto face, looked like a black gazelle as he bounded to third standing up. But his triumph was brief. Slapping his glove urgently, the Yankee second-baseman called for the ball, caught it and smugly stood on the bag. The umpire's arm shot out as if to detach the hand. "Runner is *OUT!*" he bawled.

Castinez was downcast when he stepped into the dugout. "I thought I touched the base," he said. "It was all this mud, on my shoes."

Bratton smiled and put his arm over Castinez's shoulder. "You crazy Catholic," he said in a low tone. "But anyway, you tied it up."

The game went into extra innings and if Bratton had any doubt about Deborin's acquaintance with the game, they were dispelled in the top of the eleventh. Ken Powers, who had gone hitless in the first game and got on base in the second only through a Yankee error, banished one ball from the game forever. Quite possibly unseamed, it hurtled over the towering fence as if determined to try for the Harlem River while Deborin put his hands to his head, groaned and gave the bench a vigorous kick.

Seeing him, Bukharov groaned too, and uttered a Russian curse as the players stared in awed admiration at Powers, and Bratton hustled out of the dugout to greet him. Beadle opened his mouth to free a whoop but stopped at the sight of the Russians.

"You guys crazy?" he said.

"Such excellence of striking the ball," Deborin sighed, "and all wasted."

"What d'you mean, wasted?"

"The ball—it has vanished."

"For God's sakes, we got a homer! We won the game!"

Deborin watched the players file out to shake Powers' hand. "We have made the point?"

"Even when the ball is gone?" Bukharov asked.

"Oh, brother," Beadle said. "It's a homerun! We beat 'em, don't you understand, we win!"

Beadle started to unbutton his shirt. "By the way," he said, "how's your daughter?" Deborin just glared at him, and said nothing.

When Bratton returned from the showers, Deborin and Bukharov were waiting near his locker. He noticed that for the first time since his arrival Bukharov, though still unsmiling, looked a little less unpleasant. Bratton himself was in good spirits for the Sox had split the four-game series while Cleveland was routing Detroit. Now the Sox were in sole possession of third place, six games from the Yankees and three behind the second-place Baltimore Orioles; but Detroit had fallen to fourth, seven games behind the pace.

"Tonight," Deborin said, "we have a meeting in your hotel, after supper."

"Another conference?" Bratton said, slipping into his trousers.

"You will teach me tonight the sport of baseball. I wish to know everything."

Bratton buckled his belt and smiled. "I've been in it a long time, and I'm still learning. You want to learn it all in one night?"

"There is not much time. We must proceed with quickness."

"All right. I'll do the best I can."

"You will find me a good student. Your Mr. Dewar, he will bring to me the cards from the gums. I will study them much and bring them to the meeting."

Bratton had heard of the cards. "I meant to tell you about that," he said. "You won't need them. I've copied all the information down in a special book I keep. It's a lot simpler than carrying all those cards around."

"That is good. You are much alert, like a true deputy chairman."

As they were leaving, Bratton said: "I would appreciate it, Mr. Deborin, if we could skip that deputy chairman business."

"Your title, you do not like it?"

"Well, it doesn't sound right for baseball."

"You would prefer foreman?"

"Hell, no."

"Shop controller?"

"That's not what I had in mind?"

"I suggest, then, collective planner?"

"That isn't it, either. You see—"

"I have it! Supervisor of the personnel."

"You don't understand. I figure—"

"Mr. Bratton, you must find a title and then like it. I would say, then, director of production."

"No. All that stuff's okay in your factories back home. But this is a baseball team."

"Then I wait your thought."

"I think assistant manager would be all right."

"Assistant manager, hmmm . . . Then I am the manager, yes?"

"Yes, Mr. Deborin," Bratton said. "You're the manager."

Bratton hadn't really minded the idea of a meeting in his room. The team had a Monday layover, anyway, before opening in Baltimore for the windup of the road trip.

He wondered, though, if Deborin ever went anywhere alone. At the game, this afternoon, he had brought Bukharov with him (or had Bukharov brought him?). He had him in tow again tonight. And Ambassador Galynin was along, too. And so was Tasia.

But he was grateful for Tasia's presence. With all those dour Russian faces around, it was a relief to have a pretty girl in the group. He sneaked the quick, practiced look of the middle-aged male at her legs, as she sat, and decided they were just the way he liked legs on a girl.

He was pleased, too, that Mike Dewar was on hand. Good old Dewar, who had thought of the blackboard to illustrate the bull session and ordered vodka to soothe the Soviet breast.

Deborin lost no time proposing a toast. "I drink to our glorious union," he said, raising his glass. Neither Dewar nor Bratton was sure if the reference was to the Soviet Union or the ball team, and they didn't care to ask.

After more toasts, to Childers' memory and Baltimore's defeat, Bratton suggested as delicately as he could that Bukharov, at future games, might enjoy himself more in the stands. He sweetened the proposal by offering to supply the tickets, but Deborin wouldn't hear of it. He needed Bukharov as a consultant, he said, and Bukharov's place was in the dugout.

"But we're a little crowded down there," Bratton protested. "After all, there's twenty-five players on the roster; then there's the coaches, the trainer, the batboy, and—"

"What you call the batboy," Deborin interrupted, "that is necessary?"

Bratton assured him it was.

"Your Voice of America," Bukharov sneered, "it does not tell us that you have still child labor in this country. This was abolished in the Soviet Union many years ago."

Patiently, Bratton and Dewar explained the child labor laws. It was a revelation to the Russians that not only was young Jerry Thiel's education not neglected, but he would be entering college on a sports scholarship. Apparently satisfied, Deborin raised a glass again. "I drink to your children," he said.

Bratton noticed that on each toast the Russians, except for Tasia, downed their glass. He would have preferred sipping but he felt etiquette ordered that he follow suit. The glasses were refilled. "And I drink to your children," he said.

Dewar felt a new courage warming up his blood, poured himself another and glanced slyly at Tasia. "I'll drink to your child anytime, Mr. Deborin," he said. Deborin was silent, but a soupçon of a blush brushed Tasia's cheeks.

Bratton drew a baseball diamond on the blackboard and reconstructed the afternoon plays at Yankee Stadium to dramatize his lecture. His discourse on the homerun fascinated the group, especially Deborin who inquired about the distance of Powers' blow.

"It cleared the fence," Bratton said, "and at that point the fence is three hundred and twenty-five feet from the plate."

"The fences are the equal distance in Chicago?" Deborin asked.

"No. All parks aren't built the same. At Comiskey Park, the fences are four hundred and fifteen feet at center field, and three hundred and fifty-two at left and right."

"You said Komisky," Galynin interrupted. "This is Russian?"

"No," Bratton smiled. "The Comiskeys are an old Irish family. They founded the Chicago White Sox."

"Once when I was Ambassador to Turkey," Galynin went on, "there was in my employ a translator who was called Anasta Komisky. He was not an Irish. He was a Russian."

Deborin was impatient. "It is more important to discuss the fences," he said. "In Chicago, we shall move them closer."

"What for?" Bratton asked.

"So our club will strike more hammers."

"Homers," Dewar said unsteadily.

"We'll get more homers," Bratton said, "but so will the other guys."

"I would not have thought this," Bukharov said, trying to ease the awkward moment.

"'Course not," Dewar giggled. "Why don't you propose a toast to the homer and sickle?"

Bratton was embarrassed but, surprisingly, Galynin seemed amused. "I drink to your Mr. Powers," he said.

Bratton excused himself and went to the bathroom where he poured out the vodka and replaced it with water. When he returned, he ticked off the roles of each position on the field. This done, Tasia was puzzled on one point: "I do not understand why you need three bases. It would be simpler, would it not, with only one base three times as long?"

Bratton explained that this would eliminate about ninety per cent of the action, including the excitement of running, sliding, the pickoff and base stealing.

"They steal the bases?" Deborin said in disbelief.

"We got the smartest base stealers in the league," Dewar said, pointing the bottle at the Russians.

Bukharov leaned into Deborin's ear again. "It is the mark of decadence in this country," he said, looking to Galynin for approval. "Crime is everywhere."

"And now we learn it is even in the athletics," Galynin said sadly. "This is very serious."

Again Bratton had to explain, and again his monolog was climaxed by a toast, and again Bratton prudently went to the bathroom for water. "To the glorious pilferers of the bases," Deborin said, when Bratton returned.

"You lost me there," Dewar said happily, "but I'll drink to that."

When the meeting broke up, Bratton said he hoped Deborin had learned some basics of the game.

"I learn something tonight," Deborin said at the door.

"I learn you know your subject much. I shall have confidence in my absence."

"Your absence?" Bratton wondered.

Deborin disclosed he wouldn't accompany the team to Baltimore because he would be busy with arrangements to take up residence in Chicago. The ambassador had already enlisted the help of the attorney Leonard Daniels (now on the committee running the Russian-owned Childers project) and Daniels had assigned a Miss Wiley to turn the Presidential suite of the Childers-Chicago Hotel into a home for the Deborins. Bukharov and two Russian bodyguards, Galynin revealed darkly, would occupy an adjoining suite.

"Bodyguards?" Bratton said. "You're joking!"

"We do not make the joke," Galynin said, with some tartness. "We have done much reading of Chicago and we know of the situation of the gangsters there. My government is taking all precautions for the safety of Mr. Deborin and his daughter."

After they left, Dewar spread himself on the couch and closed his eyes. Bratton loosened Dewar's tie and took off his shoes. Then he removed the glasses and bottles and, undressing, began to think about Baltimore and the Orioles. He also wondered about the team meeting that Beadle, as player representative, had called for next week. And he hoped that Deborin's first public appearance, in Comiskey Park, would be free of incidents.

With an effort, Dewar opened one eye and laughed. "To the glorious pilferers of the bases," he said. "Piffle!" Then he fell asleep.

5

Miss Wiley gave the ruffles on the new drapes a last, satisfied pat and stood back to admire them once more. She was proud of her selection and certainly Mr. Deborin would find them exquisite, too. He was, after all, a man with sporting blood; surely he would appreciate the plain gray pattern with the white stripes ever so much more than that garish red-flower thing she had taken off the windows.

In fact, Miss Wiley was proud of all the changes she had made in the suite. She especially liked the new bedspreads and towels, and the green rug in Miss Deborin's bedroom—which was no longer a hotel bedroom; the new rug, so thick it seemed to caress her heels, and the teak chiffonier had transformed it into a dainty boudoir. The suite, indeed, was gone and a home had taken its place.

She was tired, now, but that didn't matter because the hectic days had been worth it; in a sense she had prepared for this a long time. So often (it seemed very long ago) she had planned the décor of a home—her home. She remembered, wistfully, that it had been many years since she had thought about it but, strange, the drapes she had bought today were the drapes that had fluttered in the dreams she once had.

It had been so much fun, these past few days in the stores, pretending . . .

Abruptly she turned off the lights and the reverie went

out, too. There was one last thing to get, though, the surprise that would gladden the hearts of the Deborins. The idea had come to her when Mr. Daniels had mentioned the Lenin portrait hanging at the top of the winding stairway leading to the Gold Room in the Russian embassy building. One like it, Miss Wiley was sure, would go well above the fireplace.

At the art gallery the thin, bloodless young man with the tight trousers looked at Miss Wiley as if she clashed with the treasures on the walls.

"I wonder," she said timidly, "if you have a Lenin."

"Lenin?" the man said, putting a very white finger to his chin. "Lenin . . . Let's see, now. Contemporary?"

"I beg your pardon?"

"Is he modern?"

"Oh, no," said Miss Wiley, a little flustered. "He's been dead a long time."

"Odd, I can't seem to place him. What's he done?"

Miss Wiley gave him an indulgent smile. "You're pulling my leg, aren't you?"

The long white finger poked around, apparently looking for lint. "I'm sorry, madam. Maybe I can help you if you tell me what he painted."

"He was the Russian leader," Miss Wiley said. "He invented communism—I think."

The finger came down and the young man backed away. "Communism?" he gasped. "We don't have anything like that here!"

At the next shop the manager, a jowly man with lips almost browned from cigars, listened politely to Miss Wiley's request. Then, in a high, whining voice that carried all over the store, he said: "What in the world you going to do with a picture of Lenin?"

The stares of several customers distressed Miss Wiley. "It's for friends," she said.

"Friends, ha!"

Miss Wiley was sure his belch of smoke would smell up

her hat for days. "It's a housewarming gift," she tried, meekly.

"We don't carry Commie merchandise," the manager said, noting the approving glances from the other customers. "This is a respectable place and our clientele—"

Miss Wiley was into the street again, clutching her purse too tightly, as if that might smother her embarrassment. At the third shop, she decided to be brazen about it. "I have some friends from Russia," she blurted, "and they're visiting here. They're Communists and I'd like to get them a portrait of Lenin. It's very important to me. Do you have one?"

She was taken aback by the graciousness of the lady in the long blue smock. They had no such picture, the lady said, but she knew of a store that might. It was a long bus ride away and Miss Wiley decided to make it her last call. If they didn't have it, she would settle for a Russian scene; the steppes, perhaps, or maybe Red Square in the winter.

The tired old man in the worn-out slippers had no Lenins but under a layer of dust, in the studio at the back, she found an excellent substitute. Better, even, than the steppes or Red Square in the winter. Mr. Deborin would take one look and his homesick heart would swell with pride.

Mr. Deborin took one look and his jugular vein swelled with rage.

"Take that off!" he bellowed. "Immediately!"

Miss Wiley was crushed. "But I thought you would like it," she said.

The two bodyguards who had been examining their own quarters burst into Deborin's apartment. "Take it out of my eyes!" he ordered. "Throw it in the dispose of refuse."

"Oh, dear," said Miss Wiley. She was afraid she was going to cry.

"Disgraceful!" Deborin snorted, throwing his briefcase on the bed. He didn't even notice the drapes.

Bukharov, who had been directing the bellhops with the

luggage, watched the two men take down the picture. "Evidently," he said, "Miss Wiley does not read the newspapers."

"Gracious," Miss Wiley said, her chin beginning to tremble, "what ever have I done?"

Tasia took Miss Wiley's hands into hers. "Please do not worry one more minute about this," she said. "It is not your fault. It is a honest mistake. You have made this place very beautiful."

In the elevator the young man at the throttle watched the two Russians stand the picture between them. "Who's the old geezer with the pipe?" he asked. One of the men eyed him coldly, and ordered: "Take us to the basement." His companion gently turned the frame until the stern face with the pipe clenched in its mouth was facing the wall.

Because several players had arrived late at the field, Bunny Beadle conducted his meeting while they changed into their uniforms in the locker room. Commissioner Kirk and Arnold Lang, president of the American League, in Chicago to witness Deborin's debut, had accepted Beadle's invitation to attend.

Beadle was not especially fond of Kirk who always referred to him as "that union organizer," a term he despised, instead of player representative. But he was glad that Kirk was present because most of his remarks were directed to the commissioner and to Lang.

As he stood on the bench facing his teammates, Beadle realized he was offering few, if any, recommendations that could be followed through. It was more a cry of frustration than a directive, more complaining than constructive. He couldn't very well tell the players to walk out, since there was no other place for them to work. He couldn't even suggest a slowdown, for jeopardizing the race for the pennant would be blowing the team's chance at a share of the World Series purse.

For the most part, then, his only recourse was to keep

harping on the theme that the White Sox, with a man from the Kremlin at the helm, were the laughingstock of baseball. He called on Kirk to do something, anything, to put an end to a situation that had become intolerable, winding up with the clincher he had used on the players individually: "Don't forget it for one minute—no matter how they explain it, you and I are working for a bunch of lousy Communists."

Kirk mounted the bench to sympathize with the plight of the players, but he had to admit he was powerless to do anything to rectify the injustice. "I've even been asked to find a way to pull the Sox out of the American League," he said. "So I do that. So you're out of a job and the whole thing's up for grabs. How do we finish the season with just nine teams in the League? And where does that leave you guys? I'll tell you where: out on your fannies. So don't let's get panicky. Finish off the season and just give your commissioner's office time to work things out. You have my promise things won't be this way next year."

Lang said he had just one thing to say: "Did you notice what's happened since all this started? Sell-out crowds in New York and Baltimore. Right this afternoon they're coming by the busload from as far as Milwaukee and St. Louis. The park's jammed full and they're turning 'em away by the thousands. Nothing like this ever happened in baseball; it's fantastic. You've got the biggest crowd-puller the game has ever known. If I was you fellows I'd do like the commissioner says."

Bratton's speech was the briefest. "All right," he said. "Everybody on the field."

As he threw the last pitch of his warmup—he was going against Boston—Reeves saw Tasia and Miss Wiley following an usher into the team's box between home plate and third base. He stuck his glove into his back pocket, took off his cap, passed an arm over his soggy blond hair, walked over to the box and introduced himself.

"We were supposed to meet at the airport the day you came in," he said. "But I got lost in the shuffle."

"Mr. Dewar told me you were there," Tasia said. "It is very kind. You are hot, yes?"

"It'll get hotter later on. I always have trouble against Boston."

"I hope very much you win."

"Thanks. This your first time at a game?"

"Yes. I am excited."

"It's the first time for me, too," Miss Wiley said. "I'm so ashamed, I can't answer her questions."

As Reeves explained his job a Boston player lofted a practice foul that fell uncomfortably close to their box, and Tasia gripped Reeves' arm in fear. The gesture gave him a warm, cozy feeling and on a sudden impulse he said: "If we win, can we celebrate at dinner?"

Tasia gave him a winsome smile then looked away, shyly. "I will speak with my father," she said. "If he says yes I cannot stay long. In the morning, Miss Wiley takes me to the shops and we will be all day there."

"Isn't it exciting?" Miss Wiley trilled. "She's getting new outfits and she wants me to help her."

"That's great," Reeves said. "By the way, where is your father?"

"He is putting on his costume," Tasia said. "Oh, look! There he is."

A mighty roar rose from the stands, but it was a blare of cruel laughter. Turning to see what the hilarity was about, Reeves was stunned by the sight of Deborin. The Russian had on only the pants of his uniform and as he strolled out to meet the Boston manager the leggings, flapping in the wind, barely covered the wide yellow garters around his calves. For the rest, Deborin wore a black shirt, a black tie, and black shoes. Reeves was mortified, for Tasia's sake.

"I'm awfully sorry," he said. "They shouldn't laugh like that."

"I understand," she said. "But it is his fault. When Mr. Dewar brought the costume to the hotel, my father did not like it. I told him he must wear it anyway. And now, look . . ."

When he returned to the dugout Deborin, to the players' surprise, seemed only mildly concerned about the scoffing in the stands. While Bukharov glowered behind him, he explained to Bratton that the Sox shirt was itchy on his skin, and he saw no need to wear cleated shoes since he didn't intend to run around the bases. The pants were a compromise because the bench was usually dirty.

Nor was he upset by Bratton's report on Beadle's meeting. "After the engagement I will speak to our athletes," he said, adding that Bratton should get Kirk and Lang to attend that meeting, too.

Reeves did not have his control as, unaccountably, was often the case against Boston and in the fourth inning, after he had allowed three successive runs, Deborin ordered Bratton to take him out of the game. Deborin's intuition surprised Bratton, and pleased him. Before going to the showers Reeves paused where Deborin was sitting and smiled wryly. "I told your daughter I'd take her to dinner if we won," he said. "That wasn't a good start."

Deborin, squinting toward center field, seemed preoccupied with something else. "It is better you go in bed and repose yourself," he said, as if talking to himself. "But I permit your hope. You will come at seven o'clock exact."

Then he touched the shoulder of Nick Dorsey, the trainer, who was busy peering into a pair of binoculars. "You all the time are looking at the audience," he said. "What is it in the seats that is so interesting you do not look at our engagement?"

"Signals," said Dorsey, immobile, like a pointer.

"Signals?"

"Yeah. In the bullpen."

"I do not understand."

Dorsey set the binoculars down on the ledge of the dugout. "Our spotter," he said. "One of the pitchers we don't use much, making like he's warming up. He studies their catcher's signals, see, then he relays 'em to our third-base coach out there. He tips off the batter."

"But the man in the bullring—uh, bullpen, how does he advise our coach?"

"Easy. He puts up one hand, or the other, or he scratches his ear or he touches his shirt. These movements tell the coach something. Here, take the binoculars. See? Watch Boone, leaning on the fence."

Deborin looked through the glasses. "I see him," he said. "He is blowing the nose in the handkerchief. This means something?"

"He's got a cold, I guess. Don't mean nothing. Keep looking."

"Now he touches the hat."

Dorsey smiled smugly and motioned toward the coach. "Watch for a fast ball," he whispered.

A fast ball it was.

"The laws of the sport," Deborin said, "they permit this?"

Bratton had overheard the conversation and walked over. "It's not what you'd call legal," he said. "But everybody does it."

"But it is spying!" Bukharov said. "You Americans, you spy in everything?"

"I wouldn't call it that. It's just a little strategy."

"I say it is cheating," Deborin said.

"But all the teams do it," Bratton said. "You just make sure you don't get caught at it."

"It is dishonest," Deborin insisted, "and I will not permit. I go now to stop it." With that, he stepped out of the dugout and marched to the plate umpire, Len Hilts, as a new wave of laughter rocked Comiskey Park. "Please I demand," he said, "a moratorium."

Len Hilts took off his mask. "You demand what?"

"A moratorium."

The umpire's face was a sweat-drenched blank.

"A moratorium," Deborin repeated. "I wish some delay in the engagement."

"You mean time out? My God, why don't you say so? Okay. Time out!"

Ignoring the hoots and jeers of the crowd, Deborin broke into a brisk trot all the way to the far fence. He stopped in front of the bullpen. "You," he shouted at the open-mouthed Boone, "the ball pitcher who is spottering. I am the chairman of the organization of the White Sox and I announce that I dismiss you from this engagement. I do not wish my athletes to spotter! You will go to the costume room and undress!"

Before he reached the dugout again, pausing to wag his fingers in the face of the third-base coach, word of what he had done passed from mouth to mouth with astonishing speed, and a strange thing happened. Hand-clapping started in the center-field area, sparse at first, then it spread into the bleachers and to the other stands as if carried on the wind, increasing in volume until a crescendo of wildly slapping palms echoed beyond the walls of the park.

Bratton noticed that Deborin seemed touched by the tribute, but neither man said a word.

Trailing five to one in the bottom of the ninth, and with two away, Bratton had about given up hope. "I'm going to use Joe Britt as a pinch-hitter," he told Deborin.

"What is this, pinch-hitter?" Deborin asked.

"Britt's my last hope. He hits in the clutch."

"Let us hope our opponents have no one there."

"Where?"

"In the clutch."

They did; Britt flied out. But since the Yankees and Orioles had also failed, Chicago lost no ground.

After the players had showered and dressed, Deborin surprised them by walking in with Tasia and Miss Wiley, who was so uneasy about the male odors of the locker room she stood near the door, alone.

"I bring here my daughter," Deborin smiled, "to show you something you did not know maybe of the Communist villains. Sometimes they have the pretty daughters, just like the American fathers. Later I will know you more and you will know me more, but now if you look you will see the head does not have horns."

Encouraged by a few smiles, Deborin then said it was proper for the men to voice their protests at meetings. "In my homeland we have many meetings always," he said. "We have no time for war because we are busy always with the meetings."

This provoked more smiles and Deborin told the players that if anyone was unhappy he should feel free to leave the club, though he hoped no one would. Several looked at Beadle, but none came forward; Beadle sat stolidly on a stool, glancing sometimes at Tasia who now had gone to stand near Miss Wiley.

"I am happy all will stay," Deborin went on, "because now all can share in much good things. These things come after I have studied very closely the situation of finance of the organization. It is good, but my government does not have interest in making the profit from activities of sport."

Then, as the men broke into broad grins, Deborin told them he was raising by five thousand dollars the salary of every member of the club, regardless of position and seniority.

"Also," he continued, "there will be a same incentive for all if our organization is triumphant to receive the glorious honor of—how you say it—the pennant. Also a same incentive if we are victorious in the heroic encounter of the World—the World Cerise."

Before the gasps and whistles had subsided Deborin pushed on, this time looking directly at Kirk and Lang. He said he had been shocked by the spying on signals in the stands, and hoped that what he had done would inspire the commissioner's office to abolish dishonesty in baseball completely. If the authorities did not move quickly on this rascality, he warned, he himself would denounce it through the press. "The public will be unhappy to learn that these things happen," he said.

Next, he explained that on television in the hotel that morning he had seen a commercial in which Ken Powers endorsed a cigarette, and on his way to the park he had seen a billboard on which outfielder Larry Oakes praised a razor blade. "You will go to your cabinet," he told the startled Oakes, "and bring to me your equipment of the shave."

Oakes returned with an electric razor. "Is that not dishonest?" Deborin said. "You say well about the shave blades, but you use the electric machine. And Mr. Powers, you are a hero to children for I see your picture in the bubble cards of the gums. It is shameful that children see you say good things about the cigarette smoking. This is example that is not good."

Oakes and Powers looked at the ground and said nothing as Deborin announced that, effective immediately, the endorsement of products by any player was forbidden.

Leaving the park in Bratton's car, Kirk said: "I'm going to be sick when the other teams hear about this."

"He comes out against stealing signals and fake commercials," Lang said, "and he's for kids having healthy lungs. You can't knock that."

"And he gives away money," Bratton chuckled. "Try knocking that!"

At seven o'clock sharp, Reeves was at the door of the Deborin apartment. "We are ready," said Deborin, putting on his hat. "Let us proceed to dinner."

6

It might have been coincidence, but the extra money promised to the players—what Deborin called "production incentives"—seemed to have a dramatic effect on the team's power at the plate in the weeks that followed. As it did each summer, the legend_____ leading the league on the Fourth of July v_____ pennant continued to intrigue most baseball_____ some were tempted to renounce it by mid-n____ the Sox returned from a sixteen-game swing _____lis, Kansas City, Detroit, and Los Angeles. B_____ came off the road with a two-game gain on _____ and, with Baltimore slumping—eight games _____were now lodged solidly in second place and c_____ games behind New York.

Almost as sta_____ re the crowd turnouts wherever the Sox played. For the first time in anyone's baseball memory a team was drawing turn-away attendance at afternoon games, and at Comiskey Park in Chicago not only were there no reserved seats left through the end of the season, but an astounding number of fans were mailing in their checks for next year. Excitement reached such a pitch that, at one count, eleven Chicago nightclubs had taken to closing their doors on nights that the Sox were at home and, in one week alone, four department stores reported that they had run out of television sets.

It went into the record that on the night of July 17, when

the Sox opened a stand against the Cleveland Indians, only three aldermen showed up at a regularly scheduled meeting of the Chicago City Council. Of these, two were die-hard Cub fans and the third had a high blood pressure that made baseball games a hazard. Next day, the mayor moved that henceforth, when the Sox were in town, all Council sessions be held in the morning; the motion passed without a dissenting vote.

Except for agitation among some extremists, conflict over the presence of Russians in the national pastime was starting to show signs of petering out. When a player made an error there no longer were shouts of "Send him to Siberia!" Deborin's dramatic display of anger on discovering that his own team was indulging in sign stealing had blossomed into a magnificent gesture of public relations. So had his order forbidding the endorsement of products, an incident that had leaked out of the clubhouse and to the press, and became a controversial issue in the worlds of advertising and finance. It had moved the National Council of Parent-Teacher Associations, in annual convention in Philadelphia, to pass a unanimous resolution commending "Commissar Deborin for his thoughtful and perceptive stand on the problem of smoking among young people."

As for the irresolute Commissioner Kirk, he was ecstatic: the public seemed happy, the box office was booming and he probably wouldn't have to make a decision.

Bratton was satisfied with the morale of his men, though he couldn't describe their feelings as exuberant. And he thought he knew the reason: Bukharov. It was certainly no coincidence that tensions appeared among the players only when the plump First Secretary to the Embassy showed his dour face in the dugout. There was no question about the shadow he cast over the clubhouse, and Bratton attached great significance to what had happened in Los Angeles: A sort of stomach acidity ("It figures," Beadle had jibed) had kept Bukharov confined to his hotel room all the time the

Sox were on the West Coast, and the players had been their old selves on the field again.

As for Deborin, Bratton felt the Commissar was adjusting admirably to his strange new task, and had made surprisingly good progress in learning the game. While at the beginning he had seemed intent on winning solely for the glory of the Soviet Republic, now he seemed to be enjoying each contest for the thrill of the play and the challenge of outwitting rival managers.

Sadly, he still refused to wear the team uniform though in a form of compromise he had condescended to wear the cap. But the black suit, black shirt, and black tie remained his trademark, moving the sportswriters to inflict on him the title of "Debonair Deborin."

More gratifying, to Bratton, were the indications that Deborin was becoming aware of his shortcomings on the field and, while not abdicating his leadership, he seemed increasingly inclined to leave the strategy decisions to Bratton. Strained at the start, their relationship was becoming more friendly and it was obvious that Deborin held Bratton's ability in high regard. He seemed no longer concerned with remaking the game or changing the rules, and had even dropped his proposal for a fifty-game schedule. When Bratton casually mentioned the apparent change in attitude, Deborin shrugged and said:

"Such matters I leave to Bukharov. My responsibility, in Moscow, is to win as many engagements as possible. But the attitude of Bukharov, it is not changing. He is still opposed to so many engagements, and especially to two engagements in one day. Also, he opposes the use of so many judges."

"But the game needs four umpires," Bratton said.

"The opinion of Bukharov is that this is typical of you Americans—you are afraid to accept the judgment of one man. In Russia, we often accept the judgment of one man."

"Well, we don't, Commissar. That's why we've got a House of Representatives and a Senate in our Congress. And you can tell Bukharov for me that's why we hate dictatorships."

Deborin gave him a strange smile. "I think it would be more interesting," he said, "if you tell him yourself, Mr. Bratton."

As he did each Friday, Mike Dewar, travel secretary, publicity director, and man of all duties brought the players' mail into the clubhouse as the team prepared for the first of a four-game series with the Kansas City Athletics. Usually the mail consisted of a few hometown newspapers and a trickling of fan letters, but this time Dewar carried a pouch, and it was full and heavy with dozens of rolled-up newspapers. "Talk about hams," he huffed, dumping the sack on the trainer's table. "Now you're clipping reviews from every paper in the country."

But these were not ordinary newspapers. As the players ripped open the tight, brown wrapping, out fell copies of *The Daily Worker*—one for each member of the team, down to Jerry Thiel, the batboy.

There was consternation, then unbelief, among the players. "Why would they be sending us this stuff?" Reeves wondered.

"Beats me," said Bratton. "It's probably somebody's idea of a joke."

"Some joke!" Beadle snorted, leafing through his copy. "There's no sports section in this crummy rag—nothing but propaganda."

Reeves was puzzled. "I thought this thing folded long ago," he said.

Bratton studied the datelines and smiled. "It did," he said. "If you guys read this, and stop looking for your names, you'll see it's the British edition."

"All the way from there," Reeves said. "How's that for brainwashing?"

At this moment there strode into the clubhouse George Crossore, the lanky, sad-eyed sportswriter from Kansas City who had accompanied the Athletics to Chicago. Crossore was the columnist who had been bruised and trampled during the melee that greeted Deborin's arrival at the airport earlier in the season, and he had been touchy about the Sox ever since. He gazed at the scene in silence for a few moments, blinked once and walked out of the clubhouse. The next day his column began:

"In my time, I have seen some strange things in baseball, but the sight that greeted me in the White Sox clubhouse in Chicago yesterday is one that I'll not soon forget. One hour before game time there stood the manager, Horace Bratton, reading *The Daily Worker*. Next to him stood Ken Powers, one of the game's all-time hitters, reading *The Daily Worker*. Leaning against a locker was 'Gentleman Jim' Reeves, the Sox's star pitcher, reading *The Daily Worker*. Sitting on the bench were Bunny Beadle, their second baseman, and Larry Oakes, their right fielder, and Jim Nelson, their third baseman and all the others—even their downy cheeked batboy—reading *The Daily Worker*. It may be in order to ask: What gives?"

The column went on from there to quote Lionel Harris, counsel for the baseball commission, as being "shocked beyond belief" at what Crossore had reported, and suggesting that "this whole odorous mess be investigated by the Un-American Activities Committee." It also quoted Calvin Eirol, head of the powerful anti-Communist organization, The Constitutionalists, as demanding that the government "immediately cut off this Red cancer in our midst."

Within twenty-four hours the White Sox were back on page one again. Bratton was furious. "I've got one arm," he stormed at Dewar, "a wife that resents my traveling, a god-awful race for the pennant, and a team that's owned by the Kremlin. And now some crackpot wants me and my men investigated. How unlucky can one guy get?"

"I think it'll blow over," said Dewar. "We got the people with us, and they'll laugh this thing away."

"I don't want to wait that long," said Bratton, "and besides this thing is nothing to laugh at. You're the publicity director; think of something."

"The first thing we'll do is issue a statement from you disavowing the whole business."

"That's a start, but it isn't much. All I can say is that I don't know a damn thing about it. That isn't a very thrilling statement."

"Then we'll get Deborin to make a statement. He told you he had nothing to do with it."

"Yeah, but he also told me he doesn't want to get mixed up in it. He didn't say it in so many words, but I think he figures Bukharov is behind the stunt and I get the feeling the less he has to do with Bukharov the better he likes it."

"That would be the clincher," Dewar said, "to get Deborin to call a mass press conference and repudiate the—"

"He won't do it. I hinted around all day yesterday that's what we needed, but no dice. He's got his worries, too."

"Maybe," Dewar mused, not listening to Bratton, "maybe if we could get through to him some other way. . . ."

"What other way?"

"I was thinking—Tasia. She's a good kid, and it's obvious the old guy would do anything for her. . . ."

Dewar had no luck trying to enlist the help of "Gentleman Jim" Reeves. "Look," said the pitcher, "I'm not that close to the girl, and even if I was she's too nice to be pushed into the middle of this thing. I've had just two dates with her, and her father and I get along well. Why should I embarrass her, and put him on the spot with his bosses back home?"

"You wouldn't be embarrassing her. You'd be helping fix up her old man's image."

"Sure, he'd have a great image here, but what's going to happen to his image back home when they send for him? No, thanks, the whole idea makes me feel like a conspirator, or something."

"Jim, you're my last hope."

"I'm not your last hope! You know who's the man for this

job? Beadle. And you know why? He's the player representative on this team; it's his job to do something about team
problems. Tasia would understand it more coming from a
guy like him—those Russians always work with people's representatives and workers' representatives and things like
that. Did you ever think of it that way?"

"No," said Dewar, "I didn't."

At first, Beadle was adamant. Why should he do anything
to make Deborin look good? Deborin was a Commie, and
once a Commie always a Commie.

But, Dewar argued, it was not a matter of making Deborin
look good. It was a matter of making the team look good,
to pull it out of this embarrassment. Besides, Beadle had
long been squawking about the Commies taking over the
team, now was the time to do something constructive about
it, to show that the players were just good American citizens
trying to do a job.

"And let's face it," Dewar wound up, "as player representative, this is your duty. It takes a lot of guts, but it's your
duty."

Beadle relented. "If you put it that way," he said, "I
guess I can go along. But how do we go about it? I just
can't call her and say I got something to talk about. And I
sure as hell can't ask her old man if I can date her—he and
I almost ain't talking."

As Beadle spoke, a smile of relief tilted up the corners of
Dewar's mouth. "I just got an idea," he said, "that'll make
it all look casual. There's no game Monday, and my wife
and I are taking her and Reeves to dinner Sunday night.
You dig up a date and just happen to bring her to the
same place. I'll ask you to join our table, there'll be a little
dancing and you'll get a chance to talk to her. We'll yak a
bit about *The Daily Worker* business and then you can get
her on the dance floor and tell her how much it would mean
to everybody if she could talk her old man into calling a
press conference—like the idea just came to you. That way,
it won't look like somebody put you up to it."

Adelaide Wiley stood by, a little apprehensive, as Tasia adjusted her white, tam-like hat to a roguish angle. Deborin was watching the operation in attentive silence and he always made Miss Wiley nervous, even when he was in a happy mood. Now he was frowning.

"I do not understand this," he growled. "Two times you have gone to a—how you call it—a rendezvous, and two times you buy the new dress. You must have the new dress for each time the rendezvous?"

Tasia threw back her head and laughed into the mirror. "Oh, Father," she said, "I ask you before to not call it rendezvous. That makes it sound like the people are not moral."

"I call it then the appointment."

"Not appointment. In this country it is called date."

"Date. Miss Wiley, you buy the new dress all the times you have the date?"

Miss Wiley, who had not had a date with a man in over twenty years, rubbed the tips of her fingers together as she always did when flustered. "Dear me, no," she stammered. "Not each time."

"But Father," said Tasia, "you forget that when we came to America I brought with me only three dresses. American girls have many dresses. Dozens."

"That is correct, Miss Wiley? You have dozens of dresses?"

"Gracious, no, Mr. Deborin," Miss Wiley replied. "Let me see—I have the black one with the fluffy white collar, and then I have a green—"

"Never mind," Deborin broke in. He turned to Tasia and a gentleness showed in his eyes. "If you must have the new dress for the rendez—for the date of Mr. Dewar at the dinner, I permit you."

Miss Wiley's voice was not much above a whisper: "Mr. Deborin, I hope you don't think I'm taking Tasia on a wild shopping spree. It's just that she wanted to see our big department stores, and I'm only too happy to show her around."

"I understand," said Deborin, now totally softened. "But

you must not think that it is only you that have big, nice department stores. We have also such establishments in my country. In Moscow there is a store where you find all that you wish under one roof, since a pin until an auto."

The two women walked to the door as Miss Wiley pulled on her gloves. "That sounds so interesting," she said.

Deborin took Tasia's head into his hands and kissed her softly on the forehead. "I wish you to be certain you do not buy everything," he smiled. "You must leave something for other citizens who go to the store."

The luxuries and varieties of the store had Tasia exclaiming like a child on Christmas morning. After buying the dress—a gray sheath with a narrow blue and gray belt—she became entranced with the styles in the shoe department.

"The heels are so long and thin," she said, fondling a taffy-colored pair. "Do you wear such shoes, Miss Wiley?"

Miss Wiley looked down at her own drab-brown shoes with the low, squarish heels. "Not in the daytime," she said, relieved that she didn't have to lie. "They're rather elegant for nighttime, though."

"But they do not look comfortable. Do you find them so?"

"Most women say they're not too comfortable, but they're stylish and I suppose that's all that counts."

Tasia bought the taffy-colored pair and the two went to the lingerie department where Tasia expressed surprise at the flimsiness and transparency of some of the undergarments. Miss Wiley's reaction was not surprise, but embarrassment, and she tried to conceal it.

"But one can see through this!" Tasia cried, holding up a negligee.

"It's not really improper," said Miss Wiley, "for a married woman to wear a—uh, transparent negligee."

"But it is not proper for unmarried women to buy one?"

Miss Wiley laughed. "I wouldn't say that. Single girls know they'll be married some day, probably, and it's like— well, getting ready. It's like rehearsing."

"Do you have one?"

Miss Wiley hoped her blush would not show. "Yes, I do," she said.

Tasia's smile was playful. "You are much—what is the word?—sophisticated, Miss Wiley. I am glad you are my friend."

Miss Wiley tried hard to muffle the bitterness in her voice. "After all, Tasia," she said, "I've lived a few years. I should have some sophistication."

They moved to a thickly carpeted alcove nearby and Tasia examined the little mounds of brassieres on the counter, and those worn by the papier-mâché mannequins, and she was astonished to discover some that were equipped so as to give nature an assist. She leaned toward Miss Wiley and said, in a confidential tone:

"I wish to ask you this because you understand these things and you can give me help. The first time that I had a date with Mr. Reeves, when my father went home early Mr. Reeves took me for a walk near the lake and he leaned to put on me a kiss. I told him no. That was correct?"

"Certainly it was."

"When you are out with a man for the first time, Miss Wiley, do you let him put on you a kiss?"

Miss Wiley's finger tips were rubbing together at such a pace she found it necessary to hide her hands behind her back. "Never," she said.

"Then," Tasia continued, "during the second date Mr. Reeves again leaned to put on a kiss and I told him no again. Perhaps I should have told him yes?"

"That depends," said Miss Wiley, stopping herself just as she was about to bite her lip. "If the girl feels that by this time she knows the man, and he seems to be a gentleman, it's quite proper to let him kiss her—on condition, of course, that the girl knows the man has good manners and will behave himself."

"You have let a man kiss you, the second time?"

Miss Wiley felt a flush at her temples, and a terrible sadness seized her. "On a rare occasion, yes," she said.

They walked out of the store and entered a taxi parked at the sidewalk. As the cab spurted into the late afternoon traffic, Tasia whispered: "You have many gentlemen?"

"I beg your pardon?" Miss Wiley whispered back.

"You have many friends that are men?"

Miss Wiley was embarrassed again. "Dear me, no, not many," she said, trying to think of a way to change the conversation. "Most men of my age are married, you know."

"You have perhaps one special one?"

Miss Wiley gazed wistfully out the window of the cab and fell silent. Finally she turned to Tasia and said: "There is one man whom I find rather interesting, but I haven't made up my mind about him. I was never one, you know, to rush into things."

That night, in her non-transparent nightgown covered by a non-transparent negligee, Miss Wiley finished brushing her teeth then looked into the mirror. "Adelaide Wiley," she said softly and slowly, "you are the all-time, all-American liar."

Then she lay on her bed and soon, in the darkness, she felt the tears well warmly in her eyes. And she turned her face into the pillow and prayed for sleep.

The next morning, shortly after nine, Miss Wiley was back in the department store, trying on a pair of shoes. They were red, and they had long, spiked heels. "They fit fine," she told the clerk. "I'll take them." Then she boarded the elevator to the lingerie department.

Mike Dewar's party ruse worked perfectly. Beadle had strolled into the nightclub with one of his girl friends, a statuesque redhead by the name of Irma Garvell who towered over him by about four inches, and had accepted Dewar's invitation to join his party. After the table had been cleared and the three couples had had a turn on the dance floor, Dewar set about leading the conversation into

The Daily Worker incident. He had no difficulty getting it started but, unfortunately, Miss Garvell kept steering it back to herself, her new hairdo, her job at the law office, her inability to tan and her admiration for baseball players. ("They're all pretty nice guys, you know what I mean?")

Finally, Dewar decided on action. "I've checked with my wife," he told Miss Garvell, "and she's given me permission to dance with the prettiest redhead in the place. Shall we?"

As they rose, he gave Reeves a knowing look and Reeves bowed to Mrs. Dewar and escorted her to the dance floor. Beadle looked at Tasia and then at the cold coffee in his cup. "One dance a night is about my speed," he said. "Do you mind if we just sit?"

"That is all right," Tasia smiled. "We can talk."

Beadle signaled the waiter and asked for more coffee. He gazed at her gray sheath with the narrow belt and said: "That's an awful pretty dress."

"I am happy you like it," Tasia said.

Beadle picked up the salt and pepper shakers and clinked them together for a few moments. "Look, Miss Deborin," he said, "I'm going to come right to the point. I represent the players, and it's important that you do something for them."

"Yes?"

"Yeah. We'd like you to use your influence on your father."

Tasia cocked her head playfully and a large wisp of black hair bounced gently on her cheek, and Beadle found himself noting how beautifully the little white hat crowned the thick jet locks.

"We know your father's against it," Beadle went on, "but we'd like for him to call a press conference. If he—"

A hand landed heavily on Beadle's shoulder and he turned and looked up at the tall man swaying unsteadily beside his chair. "Hey!" the man said, "I know who you are. You're Bunny Beadle!"

Beadle saw the pinpoints in the man's eyes and knew at

once that he was drunk. "That's right," he said, "nice to meet you. But do you mind? I'm busy."

The drunk ignored him and fastened his bleary gaze on Tasia. "And I know who this is," he went on, his voice rising. "That's the little gal from Russia. Fancy that!"

Beadle rose and put his hand on the man's arm. "Look, fellow," he said, "would you mind going back to your table? This is a private party."

The man pushed Beadle's hand away and now his voice was almost a yell: "What'cha giving me the brush-off for, Beadle? You mad because somebody spots you with this Commie broad?"

By now, Dewar and Reeves had heard the commotion and had come quickly to the table with their partners. Dewar tried to humor the drunk but the man pushed him away.

"Whatsa matter with you guys," he shouted. "I'm a Sox fan and I help pay your salaries. I know you, too, Reeves. You guys getting too big for your britches?"

"It's not that, pal," Reeves said softly. "It's just that you're interfering with our party. Now be a good boy and—"

"I know the story," the drunk yelled. "You're just mad because I've spotted you with this Commie broad. You work for Commies, and you read the Commie paper between innings, and now you're on the make with a Commie broad!"

Reeves stepped forward: "Maybe what you need, pal, is a belt in the mouth."

Beadle moved quickly between the two men. "That's all we need now," he snapped at Reeves, "a pitcher with a busted hand. Let me handle this."

He turned to the drunk: "You're annoying us, mister. Now beat it!"

"Make me!"

Beadle didn't have to hit him hard. The man had just enough martinis in him to slump to the floor the moment Beadle's fist crunched on his cheek. "Now let's get out of here," Beadle said.

They rode in near-silence in Dewar's car until they reached

Tasia's hotel. As Reeves helped her out the door, she turned to the others and said: "I am very sorry for the trouble I have made."

"Don't worry about it," Dewar said. "The headwaiter told me that pest has had it coming for a long time. There won't be any trouble."

"Mr. Beadle," Tasia continued, "I—may I call you Bunny?" Beadle grinned. "Why, sure."

"Bunny, I hope you did not hurt yourself."

"Not a bit."

"And about my father. I do not understand—"

"Skip it," Beadle said. "I'm calling my own press conference."

"How's that again?" Dewar asked.

"I said I'm calling my own press conference. There's a simpler way to clear up this stink."

"I don't get it," Dewar said.

"Just get the reporters in the clubhouse an hour before game time, Tuesday," Dewar said. "I think I got an idea."

Precisely at noon on Tuesday, Mike Dewar led fourteen newspapermen (twice the number that would normally cover a game), five photographers, and two others with portable television cameras into the Sox clubhouse. All of the players were in uniform and sitting on benches along the walls. Beadle sat on the trainer's table, leaning back on his hands, his crossed legs swinging in the air. Bratton and Deborin stood apart, by the water cooler, and Dewar promptly joined them.

When the visitors had settled down, Beadle slid off the table and pushed his hands in his back pockets. "Fellows," he said, "this is going to be short. I'm not going to say much. I just want to show you something."

He took a few paces, head bowed, as if groping for words, and turned about. "There's been a lot of talk, lately," he went on, "and a lot written up about us and this thing about *The Daily Worker*. I'm sure most of you guys know it's a bunch of nonsense, but it makes a good story so you've been having a ball with it."

He walked to the water cooler, pressed a squirt of water into the paper cup and downed it in one gulp.

"In a way," Beadle continued, "I can't blame you. But everyone of us, the players, we've been hurt—and hurt badly. It's been a big fat joke, but now I want to give you the punch line."

He squeezed the cup into a ball and dropped it at his feet.

"I'm the player representative on this team, and I spent all day yesterday talking with the players, each one separate. I told them what I was going to do. Not one of them objected. The okay was—unanimous."

Beadle walked slowly to the two privies, side by side, near the water cooler, and pushed open both doors. "Gentlemen," he said, a grim smile on his face, "this is what each and every one of the White Sox players thinks of *The Daily Worker* and the Commie system."

The newsmen stopped scribbling and looked at each other, puzzled. "Go on!" Beadle coaxed. "Take a look!"

They gathered in front of the two cubicles and peered in to find a nail piercing each wall, and transfixed to the nails were sheets of *The Daily Worker,* neatly cut into six-inch squares.

A gasp went through the group. "I'll be damned," said a voice at the rear.

Beadle walked to the training table. "Now I hope this settles all this jazz once and for all," he said.

A short, perspiring man with gray hair spoke up: "Listen, Bunny, we work for family newspapers. How we going to tell this story?"

"Yeah," one of the cameramen broke in, "my network won't put this film on the air."

Now Beadle was smug. "That's your problem," he said. "Some of you guys made us look like dummies last week.

Now you have our side of the story. You're smart with words, just find a way to tell it."

He hopped back on the trainer's table, and his grin was one of triumph. "Why don't you," he said, "tell the people that we tore *The Daily Worker* into little pieces. That's the truth, ain't it?"

The short, perspiring man turned to Deborin. "As manager of the team, Mr. Deborin, do you have any statement to make on this?"

Deborin ran a hand through the shags of silver thatch. "I will say only this," he said. "This place is the place for the athletes to prepare for the engagements. It is not the place to read the newspapers." He paused, stroked his hawk-like nose, and added: "Any newspapers. In my opinion—"

The newsmen had turned away from Deborin to look at Bukharov who had come into the clubhouse, carrying his usual briefcase, umbrella, and frown. Bukharov squinted through his thick glasses at the assemblage, and went to the wall near the lockers where he hanged his briefcase and umbrella on a hook. Then he glared at the group again, mumbled "so much people, so much people," and hurried into one of the cubicles.

The door had barely closed when it flew open again and Bukharov bounded out, shouting: "Who is responsible for this!"

Beadle got off the table again. "I am," he said.

"You," roared Bukharov, "have insulted my country!"

"We've been insulted pretty good ourselves, lately," Beadle replied, his voice calm.

"You have not heard the last of this!" said Bukharov, shaking a finger in Beadle's face.

"I think we have," said Beadle. "But just in case we haven't, let me tell you this. Next week's *Daily Worker*, I'm putting in the press-box can. And the week after that, I'm putting it in the public rest rooms."

An ashen pallor came to Bukharov's face. His mouth opened and closed several times, and he went to the hook and almost pulled it off the wall as he grabbed his umbrella and briefcase. He glowered at Beadle, then at Deborin, and brandished his umbrella at the group.

"Just for that," he shrieked, "I'm canceling all subscriptions at once!"

Later, as the men walked to the dugout, Bratton took Beadle aside. "You're a weird one to figure out." He smiled

"Yeah?" said Beadle.

"I can understand that stunt in the clubhouse. But the other night—standing up for Tasia and clouting that guy. And you're the number one Commie-hater on the team."

"Well," said Beadle, "that louse called her a broad and I don't like anybody calling a dame a broad." He slapped his hand into his mitt. "She may be a Commie—but that dame's a lady."

7

At nearly every baseball season there comes a time when the day-to-day enthusiasm of a great many zealots begins to pall, and a sort of near-apathy sets in. It generally starts to show at the wane of August when cold statistics make it plain to millions that no pennant could possibly flutter in the home park this year—again. For a few die-hards there is always the hope nursed last year, and the year before last, and the ten and twenty years before that, for a miracle. Imaginations, weary from constructing all forms of impossible rallies throughout the summer, wistfully construct one more—a sudden twelve-game winning streak (hasn't it been known to happen?) coinciding with a tailspin in which the league leaders drop twelve in a row and then . . .

But miracles are a seldom thing in baseball. There are only certain phenomena, two-legged marvels with monstrous wrists and the eyes of gods who can slam a ball into oblivion or hurl it from the mound in sinuous, unnatural trajectory. Without such in the lineup there are no miracles—except maybe next year.

And so, aside from those whose heroes decidedly stand a chance of racing into the World Series, an air of indifference takes over in the sluggish prelude to autumn, and the vast army of losers turns its interest to the remembrance of vacation and the clanging of school bells and furnace repairs and the search for scarves, and football.

But on this Labor Day there was no such indifference. True, some inertia had crept into the National League since there was no way for the Los Angeles Dodgers to miss the pennant unless they fell flat on their halfway pantaloons. (Yet even here few were really insensitive because the Dodgers had been known to do just that in the past.)

What had captured the imagination of the nation, including the segment that looked on baseball as an overly dramatized waste of time, was that the Chicago White Sox, owned by the Soviet Government, managed by a Communist commissar, and beset by rumors ranging from romance (involving Tasia) to clubhouse hostilities, were within sight of the American League pennant.

As the last long weekend of the year came to a close, the team originally boycotted by some (it had failed to place a single player on the All-Star squad), derided by others and marked for the second division by many cynics had won ninety-one games and lost forty-seven, in a precise tie for first place with the New York Yankees. In Chicago several of the finer hotels, including the two inherited by Russia in May, reported that they were already booked solid for the first week of October, though World Series tickets had yet to be printed.

Nor was the pennant fever contained in the United States. It spread to South America then hurtled the ocean into Europe. In France, *"le sport américain de baseball"* dominated the sports pages. In Spain, the White Sox saga was getting as much attention as the bullfights and in England one newspaper expressed a roguish hope that the Russians might take up cricket "in order to remove some of the tedium from our national game." In a Japanese poll among school children to name the ten most admired figures, Deborin wound up in a fourth-place tie with the Emperor.

Beyond the original announcement on the disposal of the Childers estate, little had been reported behind the Iron Curtain. But the news had gone through aboard the Voice of America which had taken to leading off its broadcasts with scores and standings, and eventually the masses set off a demand for official recognition and news of their Chicago "Belye Chulki" (White Stockings). The demand was initiated by the trade unions, heaviest supporters (with twenty-five per cent of the members' dues) of the nationwide sports training program taught at the Young Pioneer Schools. Hours after the double-header triumph on Labor Day which vaulted the White Sox into first place, hundreds of Russian unionists paraded around Dynamo Stadium on the outskirts of Moscow with hastily inscribed banners that read: HAIL TO OUR BELYE CHULKI and MIR I DRUZHBA (Peace and Friendship) THROUGH THE BELYE CHULKI. The Presidium of the Supreme Soviet of the Union of Soviet Socialist Republics could not long stay silent.

Thus it was that the high mark in international recognition of the rampaging, unpredictable White Sox came with the appearance, next day, of a small box at the bottom of the back page of *Pravda*. Headlined LAPTA, it read:

> Because of the interest expressed by our readers in the glorious victories in the United States of the Chicago Belye Chulki, the sports organization owned by the people of the U.S.S.R., the nation's 10,104 daily and weekly newspapers, including *Pravda*, will henceforth report its destinies on the playing fields of America. A representative of Tass News Agency has been dispatched abroad for that purpose. His articles will begin at an early date. This development marks the first time that *Pravda* has ever recorded continuous news of sports activities.

There was a weary stoop to the shoulders of the tall man as he descended the loading ramp, his eyes watery from long hours of reading small print. Under one arm he held a large, bulky book entitled *American Encyclopedia of Baseball and Official Rule Book*, and in the other there dangled a portable typewriter, compact and flat, with the word *TASS* embossed in gold on the cover. He was thin, almost emaciated, and he carried the objects as if they were heavy burdens. As he followed the others into the terminal, he tucked the book under one arm and made a vain motion to part his disheveled, prematurely gray hair with his free hand. It had been a long flight from Moscow, and Fedor Malsynenko was in surly spirits.

Even had the trip been smooth, Malsynenko's mood would have been unpleasant for he regarded this assignment as an unspeakable humiliation. After all, he spoke fluent French, English, and German and held a degree in political science—a richer background than many other journalists at Tass News Agency which he had served faithfully for eleven years. For the last three years he had patiently awaited that opening in Tass's Washington bureau (or, at the very least, at United Nations headquarters in New York). But here he was in this vile city of stockyards and gangsters, ordered to sit in stadiums and cable reports on a bourgeois pastime about which he knew absolutely nothing. How could a man possibly make a name for himself with such trivia?

In the taxi, Malsynenko tried to find room amid the luggage for his long legs, cramped from the flight, and as he leaned forward he caught sight of the newspaper open at the sports page on the driver's seat and read the headline: NEW YORKERS HERE FOR WEEKEND SERIES. He leaned back as the cab pulled away from the terminal and rolled toward the exits. "At what time does the contest begin?" he asked the driver.

With one hand on the wheel, the driver folded the paper and offered it to him. "One-thirty," he said. "Want to read about it?"

"No," Malsynenko said, finding a hole for his legs.

The driver picked up speed as he entered the expressway and settled down for a long chat. "You catch a lot of games?" he asked.

Malsynenko's voice was curt. "I do not wish conversation," he said. "Please bring me to the Childers-Chicago Hotel—in silence." He opened his book to page 142 and held the small print to his face and his eyes, pale blue and red-rimmed, became watery again. With an angry gesture he thrust the bookmark into his pocket, wondering when the end would come to those pages of confounded rules.

At the hotel desk, Malsynenko signed the register with a tired flourish and inquired whether Mikhail Deborin was in his room.

"Oh, no," the clerk smiled. "Right now"—he cocked his head toward the transistor radio chattering from an empty mail slot behind him—"he's got two on base and we're ahead, two nothing. Talk about excitement! Nothing like it around here for years."

Malsynenko hurried to his room, showered, changed clothes and hustled downstairs to a taxi. "Take me to the baseball stadium," he ordered, "and please drive quickly. I am late already."

At the park, Malsynenko found the ramp leading to the press box barred by a chunky attendant in uniform who wouldn't let him through. "But I am a journalist!" he cried, his fatigue hurtling to the surface.

"I've got to see your press pass," the attendant insisted.

"I do not have it. It is at my hotel."

"Sorry, Mac. You can't go up there without credentials."

"But I tell you I am a journalist! I have just come from an airplane. I have not yet opened my valises!"

"Sorry. I got my orders."

Malsynenko jerked his wrist furiously out of its sleeve and looked at his watch. "I am very late already," he sulked. "May one still buy a ticket, then?"

"Why, sure. Go round front, help yourself."

"There are still some accommodations?"

"Plenty of seats."

Malsynenko's surprise at finding no queue at the box office turned to astonishment when he took his seat almost directly behind home plate amid a vast emptiness of boxes.

He stared unbelievingly at the huge swaths of vacant chairs in all areas of the grandstand and bleachers, and estimated the attendance at less than ten thousand. Where, he wondered, were the vaunted masses who supposedly all but stormed the stadiums where their heroes appeared?

Twice during the game Malsynenko tried to find the answer—from Deborin—but twice he was repulsed by two broad-shouldered ushers as he approached the Chicago dugout.

When the game was over—a drab, one-sided affair won by the New York visitors—Malsynenko made a last, valiant try to mount the railing near the dugout but this time the two ushers grabbed him as one long leg vaulted over the fence and forced him back into the chairs. "One more try like that, buddy," the larger of the giants snarled, "and out you go on your prat!"

"Swine!" Malsynenko shouted. "Vulgarities! I shall expose your filthy behavior to the world!"

Late that afternoon the tired correspondent, who had not eaten since breakfast on the plane, ordered dinner sent to his room, hastily devoured a large steak, typed (in English) his first cable to the home office in Moscow and personally delivered it to the Western Union office around the corner from the hotel. Back in his quarters he loosened his tie, removed his shoes, dropped wearily on the bed and proudly read his carbon once more:

Chicago, Sept. 5—(TASS)—There is reason to believe that sports enthusiasts the world over may have been duped by a gigantic American hoax. Fortunately, this correspondent has succeeded in discovering the fraud and the people of the U.S.S.R., at least, shall be spared the further humiliation of gullibility. I have just returned from the baseball stadium in Chicago where, if one is to believe reports of the capitalist-owned news agencies, the highly publicized White Stockings organization is claimed to have been writing new pages in the history book of sports. History or legend?

Where we have been told that tens of thousands of citizens have been unable to purchase tickets at any price for the matches, I found to my dismay a stadium in which fully two thirds of the seating areas consisted of empty chairs. There was no line of citizens awaiting entry into the arena, and it was a simple matter for this correspondent to purchase an exorbitantly priced ticket for a chair near the contest.

Not simple, however, was my attempt to gain entry. While in civilized countries journalists are welcomed to working facilities set aside for their profession, I was rudely prohibited from entering this observation point by a brutish, well-fed dolt who demanded to examine my passport and other documents—a repudiation which speaks volumes on the freedom which foreign visitors to these shores are supposed to enjoy. Within the sparsely occupied arena, other shocks awaited me. On three occasions I made attempts to approach Commissar Mikhail Deborin, chairman of the organization, to seek from him answers to the mystery of the poor attendance. On each occasion I was barbarously repulsed as I left my seat, and one felt as if all of one's movements were being closely observed by the Americans. Indeed, on the third attempt, I was physically assaulted by two ruffians in military uniform who loudly threatened me with bodily harm and expulsion should I be so bold as to again approach the underground headquarters of Comrade Deborin. I am unable to ascertain which detachment of the soldiery these sadistic oafs belong to, and while no weapons were visible, there is cause to suspect that they were armed.

During the tournament which, incidentally, the White Stockings lost in a tally of seven to four, at no time did I observe any participants of the Negro race on the field of honor. This, in the face of continued dishonest claims from American news agencies and the Voice of America that Negro athletes are on equal footing with their white counterparts in this country. One is therefore permitted a natural revulsion at the flagrant misuses of propaganda emanating from this part of the world.

Atrocious mendacity would be a more accurate phrasing

than propaganda, for even as I write this dispatch in my hotel room a radio report is telling the public that the New York aggregation was victorious in a tally of three to zero. The fact is that I and several thousand other witnesses saw the contrary. One wonders to what limits such brazen falsehoods will be utilized. As to the match itself, this correspondent was left aghast at the unruly conduct of the rabble in the audience. Time and time again the judges were hissed and jeered loudly, and subjected to terms of derision which reflected on their honesty and eyesight—a boorishness happily not permitted in the U.S.S.R.

In the matter of the actual accomplishments of the players, it is the opinion of this correspondent that—

At this point the rigors of the journey and the frustrations of the day combined to bring total exhaustion to Malsynenko, and even his own prose was insufficient to keep his eyes open. His head nodded and he wondered hazily why Comrade Deborin had not by this time answered his telephone messages. In the brief twilight of the mind that precedes sleep he saw his name in large letters in *Pravda* and *Izvestia* and *Trud* and the many other papers that would bring him prominence tomorrow, and it gave him cause to taste the thought that his new mission might, after all, lead to a more dignified post in Washington or New York. Tomorrow, perhaps, there would be a message from Moscow about his sensational journalistic debut in America. . . .

And then he was asleep, and as he slept morning came to his homeland and with it came the prominence, born of his printed word, that prompted the message from Moscow.

The message came not from cable. It came with a violent knock on the door shortly after noon that roused him from a childlike fourteen-hour sleep. He lifted his long legs quickly from the bed and, patting his rumpled suit, half-ran to the door, turned it open and threw wide his arms in a gesture of welcome.

"Commissar Deborin," he exclaimed in Russian, "at last we meet!"

The stern figure in the doorway stared through thick glasses for a long moment, then replied in the native tongue: "I am Stepan Bukharov, First Secretary to the Embassy in Washington, and you"—he stepped briskly into the room and slammed the door—"are a miserable cretin!"

Malsynenko said nothing. He was stunned and, embarrassed by his disorderly appearance, he walked a semicircle in his stocking feet and stood in the middle of the room, thumping down his ruffled hair.

"You have disgraced yourself and the agency you work for," Bukharov stormed, "and you have shamed our country!"

Malsynenko leaned down and picked up his shoes. "I do not understand, Comrade Bukharov," he said.

Bukharov walked to the divan near the window which looked onto the street and sat down. "You are surprised I am not Commissar Deborin? You wonder why you could not see him yesterday as it says today in our papers at home? You should! Commissar Deborin is one thousand miles from here!"

Malsynenko sat on the bed and forced his left foot into the shoe. "He is?"

"He is. Do you know what you did yesterday, you idiot? You went to the wrong baseball match. You were in the wrong stadium. You were observing the wrong division!"

Malsynenko, with what appeared to be an agonizing effort, put on his other shoe. "I must repeat," he said hesitatingly, "I do not understand. I reported a match between the Chicago group and the New York group and I—"

"You imbecile! You observed a match between two other groups called the Chicago Cubs and the New York Metropolitans. They are in another division, and they are of no interest to the people now!"

"Then the White Stockings," Malsynenko whined, "where are they?"

"They are in New York where they are combating the

New York Yankees. Mountains of manure! How could you do such a stupid thing?"

Malsynenko put his hands to his head and closed his eyes tightly, as if trying to shut off the world. "Oh, the shame of it!" he said. "I do not know how I could make this terrible mistake!"

"Why did you not call me when you arrived? I have quarters in this hotel."

Malsynenko began to walk the floor in long, desperate paces. "I did not know that, Comrade," he said. "I assumed you lived in Washington." He paused at the window and looked down at the bustle of Michigan Avenue. "I have disgraced myself," he went on. "My career is ruined. Certainly I shall be dismissed."

The scowl eased on Bukharov's face but the acid remained in his voice. "Perhaps I can help you," he said. "If you do as I say."

Malsynenko ceased his pacing and the first feeling of relief effaced the droop on his mouth. "I have made one unpardonable blunder," he said. "I propose not to make another. I shall do as you direct."

It was quite understandable, Bukharov explained, that a foreigner just off an airplane and in a hurry could make the mistake of hustling off to the wrong park, especially amid the confusion of two teams from Chicago playing two teams from New York. Malsynenko's first move, then, would be to immediately cable another report admitting the unfortunate error and correcting the record. From this day on, however, Malsynenko would keep in constant touch with the First Secretary, checking with him when in doubt before sending his dispatches to Moscow. In addition, since he would be constantly with the team, Malsynenko would be in an ideal position to take notice of any unusual circumstances, either in conversation or deportment, involving Commissar Deborin and his daughter, Tasia, and it would be his patriotic duty to report any untoward happenings immediately.

To be quite frank about it, Bukharov pursued (and certainly this conversation was to be held absolutely confidential), he had reason to feel that Commissar Deborin had become entirely too fraternal in his relationship with the Americans, and clearly Malsynenko would appreciate the importance of the Embassy's being fully informed of such peculiarities. Further—and this was a situation which simply could not be tolerated—Tasia had been seen (by one of her father's bodyguards) in public places with at least one of the White Stockings players.

Bukharov paused, removed his glasses and tapped his teeth with the crossed temples. Then he said suddenly: "You are married?"

"Yes," Malsynenko replied. "I have two children."

"No matter. I assume you are prepared to serve your government in any way asked of you?"

"Yes, naturally."

"Then it will be your duty to, uh—approach Tasia Deborin, become friendly with her when the occasion permits, and report to me personally on her attitude, her sympathies. You understand?"

Malsynenko's eyes became a little watery again. "I understand," he said.

Bukharov returned his glasses to his head and for the first time since entering the room permitted himself the semblance of a smile. "No doubt," he said, "this will add some —let us say—zest to your assignment."

Fedor Malsynenko smiled wanly and said nothing. He wished Bukharov would leave, so he could zest up with a shower and shave.

8

Had Malsynenko limited himself to reporting the baseball scene in the normal fashion of sportswriters, he quite likely would have been accepted by the American press corps and by the players themselves. Indeed, because of the disastrous botch he made of his first day at a ball game and the cruel handicap of knowing nothing about his assignment, many felt a surge of sympathy for the bewildered Tass correspondent. In a way he was an underdog and, like all underdogs, he had rooters who wished him well. But he quickly alienated the early sentiment by sending sociological and political essays to his Moscow home office instead of concentrating on the drama of skill and competition on the diamond.

During pre-game practice he would buttonhole players on the field and ferret their opinions on such matters as disarmament and racial segregation. Once, he trapped Ken Powers for his views on the Common Market and the friendly center fielder, who was something less than a profound thinker, admitted that he hadn't the vaguest notion on the subject. "My wife," drawled Powers, expelling an enormous spit through the batting cage, "does all the shopping." From this Malsynenko had fashioned a devastating treatise on the legend that American athletes were intellectual opaques whose characteristic was brainless brawn. The story had gained wide circulation abroad, and a domestic reprint had both embarrassed and offended a great many American readers.

Incidents like these had, in time, created a coolness between Malsynenko and the players, a coolness aggravated by his refusal to fly on out-of-town games in the team's chartered plane. Instead, he traveled in solitary snobbery aboard commercial airliners. Further, because of the tenseness he brought to the press section at Comiskey Park, he had taken to covering home games from the boxes reserved for the relatives and guests of the White Sox staff, and whenever Tasia showed up for a game (she had missed very few of late), usually accompanied by Miss Wiley, he would make it a point to sit with her. One complication in this menage was that he frequently called on the girls to explain plays he did not understand. When Tasia, who had difficulties with the basics of the game, was unable to help him Miss Wiley would volunteer her interpretation of the action with—since she understood even less—quite wretched results.

Inevitably, Malsynenko's account of one game was so outlandish—he had volunteered the advice that the players wear gym uniforms on hot days—that an American newsmagazine had translated it for home consumption and tickled its readers into a national giggle. Such was the temper of the Tass chronicles that on a flight home from Los Angeles, where a three-game sweep had thrust the surging Sox into the lead for the first time, Bratton couldn't resist ribbing Deborin about Malsynenko's quaint style.

"I don't know how your people back home can follow what's going on," he said. "Listen to this: 'The next participant struck the ball a forcible blow, then proceeded rapidly to the nearest goal.'"

Deborin's smile was indulgent. "The writing of Malsynenko is of a composition that is odd," he conceded.

"And here's more," Bratton tittered. "'After capturing the ball in flight he refused to acknowledge the applause. Instead, he threw the ball with great force at a colleague, as if in anger.' My God, how cockeyed can this fellow be?"

Deborin snapped open the briefcase on his lap and a glint of mischief played in his eyes as he reached in and withdrew a packet of newspaper clippings held together with a rubber band. "It is not good to crow too loud," he said. "Your American writers they are odd ones too."

"Maybe, but their stuff makes sense, even for kids."

Deborin rolled off the rubber band and held up a clipping. "I am one adult who is not certain," he said. "Permit me to read: 'Southpaw Earl Krope scattered four taps and his mates laced a brace of horsehide out the outer gardens. . . .' This is English?"

Bratton laughed, but he was a touch uncomfortable. "Sometimes they use corny expressions," he said, "like apple and—"

"And the pellet and the sphere," Deborin broke in. "In one newspaper it is even called the onion. And now hear this information: 'Clemson died between the keystone and hot corner, curtaining the afterpiece.'"

"He was tagged trying to reach third base," Bratton explained, "and that ended the second game of a doubleheader."

"Very interesting. And now: 'The way Soren's leaning on lumber he's lead-pipe to ink a pact next semester.' Translation, please?"

"He's batting so well he's sure of a new contract next season."

"Strange. You laugh because Malsynenko calls the bat the stick, but here it is called lumber, and the mallet, and the hickory, and the shillelagh, and the appleknocker. That is better than stick?"

Bratton leaned across the aisle and gave Deborin a playful punch on the arm, his first real gesture of affection since the two had met.

"You got a point," he grinned. "I take it all back."

Deborin returned the clippings to his briefcase, and his

smile of triumph suddenly faded as he pulled out a Russian newspaper. "I wish everything we read was as much pleasant," he said. "I have here *Izvestia*, the latest edition I have received, and I have much concern for something that Malsynenko writes."

He read quietly to himself for a few moments, as if to memorize the lines, and turned to Bratton:

"This is not good," he said. "I will say it is much shocking. In this dispatch, Malsynenko makes the protest about the Russian flag. He tells his readers that our country is in a dishonor."

Bratton leaned forward. "Flag? What's he talking about?"

"He is in anger," Deborin continued, "because the flag of my country is not in the park of baseball."

"Oh, for God's sakes. The guy's out of his skull! What's your flag got to do with it?"

Deborin folded the paper, and there was a melancholy strain to his voice. "He calls it a patriotism matter," he said, "national pride. He explains that the American flag flies at Comiskey Park at all times."

"So?"

"He says it is a disgrace that the Russian flag does not fly there also."

"That doesn't make sense!"

"To him it makes sense, and I have fear it will make sense to the readers in my country. You see, he tells in much details that Comiskey Park now is a property of the Russian government because Mr. Childers he has given it to my country."

"Holy cow! I didn't think of that. . . ."

"So you see, in the thinking one reads in *Izvestia*, Comiskey Park is Russian territory, and on Russian territory it is correct and the law that the Russian flag is to be."

By now players in the nearby seats had turned about and were listening openly to the conversation.

Bratton was speechless for almost a full minute. "I'll

be damned!" he said, finally. "Russian property. I'll be damned!"

The players stared in silence at Deborin. "It is possible nothing from this will happen," he said, apology now submersing his previous high humor. "But if trouble comes, I am much sorry."

Bratton dropped his chin into his hand and stared reflectively out the window at the darkness descending on the immense checkerboard of slate and green below. "Russian property," he repeated aloud to himself. "God!"

In the long, sexagenarian memory of Captain Timothy Stroud, chief security officer at O'Hare Field, this was the largest, happiest welcoming crowd he had ever seen at an airport. "I've seen four Presidents come and go from this place and Midway," he told the platoon of Chicago policemen called in for emergency duty, "but this beats 'em all. Can you imagine the mob if this was daytime?"

It was a little after two o'clock in the morning when the control tower finally called in the Sox plane after a stack-up above the globs of autumnal fog scudding out to Lake Michigan like eerie, dripping ectoplasm. Despite the hour and the marrow-chilling air, more than six thousand cheering, chanting fans were on hand, their fervor roused by Captain Stroud himself who decided that the sweet taste of a pennant justified his waving them to the ramp as the players disembarked.

The crowd spread forward, waving signs that read GO, GO, SOX! and A PENNANT AT LAST! and dozens broke ahead to touch the players and pound them on the back. In the gleeful melee, Bratton tugged at Deborin's arm and pointed to one sign that exclaimed WE LOVE YOU, DE-BORIN and, in smaller letters below, AND YOU, TOO, BRAT-TON! and both men laughed heartily. Several of the players' wives managed to push and twist their way into their husbands' arms and when Deborin spotted Tasia and Miss Wiley he scrambled headlong into the swirling celebrants and lifted his squealing daughter high in the air and hugged her tightly.

"You are making us feel like heroes!" Deborin shouted above the din.

"You are heroes!" Miss Wiley shouted back. She pointed beyond the crowd to the terminal entrance. "Look," she yelled, "even Bukharov is smiling. For the first time!"

And he was. As Deborin and Bratton pulled themselves away from the well-wishers and started for the terminal, Bukharov walked toward them, his hand extended.

"It is a time for felicitation," he said. "It is good to be in first position."

Deborin thanked him and Bratton nodded, his one hand in his coat pocket. Bukharov fell into step with them and as the three entered the terminal, he said: "I have acquired a banner which you especially, Commissar Deborin, will find pleasing. But I did not think I should bring it here tonight."

"Yes? said Deborin.

"Yes," Bukharov went on. "I refer to the banner of our homeland—the Red flag."

"That is interesting," Deborin said, stepping up his pace.

"It was my thought you would think so," said Bukharov. "No doubt you have read the article by Comrade Malsynenko?"

"I did."

"And no doubt you are in agreement."

"Agreement?"

"Yes, that it is shameful that the Red flag is not in Comiskey Park where the American Stars and Stripes is prominent?"

Bratton stopped suddenly and whirled to face Bukharov. "Look," he growled, "who you kidding with this flag stuff? Don't you have something better to do with your time than to keep pestering us?"

"I assure you, Mr. Bratton, that this is a very serious matter."

"And I assure you that I'm dead tired from this trip and

so is Mr. Deborin, here, and your job is in Washington so why the hell don't you stay there and keep out of our hair?"

They were at the front entrance now, and the bus chartered to convey the team to Chicago rolled slowly into position.

"I wish to make it clear, gentlemen," Bukharov persisted, "that I wish to place the Red flag in Comiskey Park, and remove the American flag."

"You try that," Bratton snapped, "and you get lynched."

"I expected this opposition from you," Bukharov said, his pudgy body beginning to shiver with the cold. "For that reason I have called a meeting for tomorrow afternoon in the office of Mr. Bradley to discuss the matter."

Bratton exploded. "A meeting? You must be out of your mind! The only meeting tomorrow's going to be a team meeting, or have you forgotten we're trying to win a pennant?"

Bukharov turned the collar of his light gray coat to his neck. "If your flag is removed from the park," he said, "there will be no games. And if there are no games"—he showed his frozen smile again—"it is foolish to speak of a pennant."

Deborin broke his silence. "Impossible!" he said. "This is a bad thing."

"Not impossible, Commissar," said Bukharov. "I must tell you that this is an order directly from Ambassador Galynin in Washington."

Deborin was shocked. "I do not believe this," he said.

"Then I suggest you ask the Ambassador himself tomorrow," Bukharov smirked, raising his hand at a passing cab. "He is flying here for the meeting."

In the office of the late Armistead E. Childers, now occupied by Herman Bradley who had been his vice-president, Adelaide Wiley felt ill at ease. She could not recall having seen so many people sitting in Mr. Childers' office—she preferred to remember it as his office—at one time. Mr.

Childers had always detested crowded meetings, chosing to confer with his executives one or two at a time.

Now the place was alive with men, angry men with angry, loud voices—some of them indelicate, even profane. It was all quite unpleasant, and two hours was altogether too long for any argument.

Bradley had instructed her to take general notes on the discussion, not a transcript, and because the Russians had the irritating habit of repeating their statements word for word there were many lulls during which she amused herself by conjecturing on the verdict if the issue should come to a vote.

Quite obviously Bukharov could count on the support of Ambassador Galynin (Did he ever stop rubbing his nose?) who wouldn't have come all the way from Washington if not to insist that the Red Star replace the Stars and Stripes in Comiskey Park. Bukharov could also count on Valentin Kononov, the trade attaché who had come in from the embassy with Galynin, though Miss Wiley couldn't imagine what business this issue was of his. He was here simply to pack the lobby, no doubt.

And there was Malsynenko, who had instigated the crisis in the first place (or had Bukharov, Miss Wiley wondered, put him up to it?).

It was decidedly unfair that Malsynenko should be permitted to sit in on the meeting when the same privilege was denied the other newsmen. But Malsynenko worked for the Russian government and the Russian government owned the team, so the other side plainly held all the cards. The party cards, Miss Wiley mused, in a humorless afterthought.

Against the flag issue, naturally, were Bratton, Mike Dewar (who looked as though he had another hangover), and Bunny Beadle, attending the conference in his capacity of player representative. Bradley, interim president of the structure set up to reorganize Childers' holdings, would have to be neutral. So would Leonard Daniels, the solemn, red-haired corporation counsel, and his fidgety aide, Tom Morris, who never knew what to do with his pipe.

So that was four of them, Miss Wiley thought, and three of us, unless Deborin kicked over the traces. But would he? Would she, if she were in his place? What if—something nagged a crowded corner of her mind, something that somehow felt like it had to be wrestled. . . .

But this was idle daydreaming. The other side had no intention of courting democracy with a vote, not with that awful Bukharov bellowing the way he was.

"I must repeat," Bukharov was saying, "that only this flag belongs in our sport stadium and we cannot accept your protests." For the third time that afternoon he marched dramatically to the wall where the flag was leaning and unfolded it with relish, exposing once more the gold hammer and sickle in the upper left corner and touching with reverence the five-point red star surmounting it.

"And I've got to repeat," Bratton said, his voice now wearied almost to a murmur, "that the public won't stand for it. We might have a riot on our hands!"

"That," Ambassador Galynin broke in, "will be the concern of you—not us." He turned in his chair and waved his pince-nez at Deborin. "We have not heard much of your opinions, Commissar," he said with a thin, fangy smile. "Surely one will expect from you comments on the directive of your government."

Deborin, who had been leaning over with his eyes on the carpet, sat up and jerked his head to throw back the silvery lock of hair that had fallen over his eyes. "Because of the directive of my government," he said, speaking slowly, "only one flag concerns me at this moment . . . It is the flag that is called here the pennant. For this it is I was sent here."

"We are not amused," Galynin said, "with this answer that makes circles near the issue."

Bukharov replaced his flag on the wall, but he did it with a nervous clumsiness and it almost slid to the floor. "Also we are not amused," he said, "with things we are hearing of you and your daughter—" He stopped, as if stunned by what he had said.

Bunny Beadle rose slowly to his feet. "One crack about that girl," he rasped, "and you get that flag down your throat—staff and all!"

Miss Wiley didn't know at all what lifted her out of her chair, but she suddenly found herself standing, her knees trembling. "Dear me," she stammered. "Wouldn't anyone like a nice cup of tea?"

"No!" Bukharov almost shouted. Galynin's nod was a no, as were Bratton's and Malsynenko's and Beadle's. The others looked at her with blank stares of disinterest.

"It's brewing in my office," Miss Wiley tried again, "and I thought—"

Amid the self-conscious silence Deborin half-stood and made a slight bow with his head. "This would be much nice," he said, with a warm smile. "I would like one tea, please."

The nagging strangeness persisted as Miss Wiley fiddled about in the outer room with cups that rattled too much in their saucers, and her hands shook more than usual, and suddenly she felt within her as if a massive, thick door before which she stood had been pulled off its hinges and a blinding light crashed in and a cool, gentle breeze tingled her cheeks and when she walked out again she was in complete control of those thin, spiked heels that all these days had twisted grotesquely into the carpet.

She gave Deborin his cup and her hand no longer trembled, and she placed hers on Bradley's desk. Then she turned to face the combatants.

"Gentlemen," she said, and it was such a rare ecstasy for her to hear the firm timbre in her voice, "the meeting is over."

In continued silence the men looked at her, then at each other.

"Gentlemen," she repeated, and she thought of restraint

now because she knew she must not spoil the moment, "the meeting is over because there is no issue."

Bukharov finally found his voice. "You will please explain," he growled, "because we have not the time, madam, to—"

"In this country," Miss Wiley said evenly, "it's not polite to interrupt a lady. The explanation will be brief." She walked to the flag and looked at its redness. Then she turned and faced the men again.

"The issue," she said, "is a demand by the Russian representatives that the Soviet flag replace ours in Comiskey Park. If Comiskey Park belongs to the Russian government, then the flag belongs in the park."

"That is correct," Bukharov said, blinking contentedly behind his thick glasses.

"But it's not correct," Miss Willey said. She saw Bukharov's mouth open again and gestured for silence. "When the Russian government announced its disposal of Mr. Childers' estate, to Mr. Bradley and the others here, it was directed that all physical properties revert to the employees of his various enterprises."

Astonishment settled on the group, and Morris' pipe dropped to the floor but no one noticed. Miss Wiley turned her face, now a little flushed, to Galynin. "I have read your government's instructions often enough to recite them from memory," she went on. "Mr. Ambassador, you will recall that you yourself delivered the stipulation that Mr. Childers' employees were to come into possession of his physical properties. Comiskey Park is a physical property, it was not sold, and therefore it belongs to the employees. It does not belong to your government, which owns only the franchise, but to the players. It follows, then, that the Russian flag cannot legally supersede the American flag of United States citizens."

It was long after the Russians had made their huffy departure—two more cups of tea later—that Deborin and Bratton finally prepared to leave.

94

Deborin paused in the doorway and took Miss Wiley's hand into his.

"Dear lady," he said, and there seemed to be a small catch in his voice, "yesterday we were the heroes. Today, you are the hero."

9

Now, as the long shadows of late afternoon lay on the outfield grass, the magic number was one.

Like coolies plodding through a rice paddy, the ground crew pulled the dragging equipment off the infield as the fifth-inning break neared its end, and "Gentleman Jim" Reeves stood tall on the mound, preparing to make his last warmup pitch a fast ball. This would probably be the day, and his only regret was that it was not happening at home.

In the dugout, Horace Bratton watched the long, supple fingers of his most devastating pitcher coil about the ball and envelop it until it disappeared, as if behind tentacles, and he felt a placid contentment. He tilted the dark glasses to the top of his head and turned to Deborin. "Now I can taste it," he said.

"Taste?" Deborin asked.

Bratton laughed softly. "We have an expression here," he said. "When you want something bad, really bad, and you wait for it a long time and then it gets real close, you say you can taste it."

Deborin smiled and some of the tiredness went from his face. "So now you taste your pennant, yes?" he said.

"You damned right. It's been a long time coming."

Bratton lifted a foot to the ledge of the dugout and leaned forward on one knee, and the gleam in his eyes was that of a boy who'd just passed his driver's test. It was as if he were talking to himself.

"We're going to make it right here. This afternoon. All day I've been feeling it."

Deborin's face assumed an air of mock determination. "But we must!" he said, forcing a poorly executed frown. "I promise Tasia this pennant will happen to us in Boston. I must keep the promise."

"Confidence like that, I like."

"But it is her which have the confidence! Before we depart Chicago she request to come with me here because she is certain that in Boston all this nice things will happen. And she said she will bring good fortune to our pennant, so I tell her come. And you see? We have the good fortune, now, and they do not have points and we have six points."

Bratton leaned over the fountain and sucked the water loudly and let its dribble roll over his chin and soak his wet, prickly collar. "I've never seen Fenway Park look so good," he said, his gaze on the netting above the low left-field fence. "I feel like I could go out there and hug everybody." He turned to Deborin and grinned, a little giddily. "Even you, Mike!"

In all the months they had been together, this was the first time that Bratton had addressed the Commissar in this fashion. Even during the intimate tensions of the crises they had shared in ball parks and hotel rooms, he had never called him in any other way than "Mr. Deborin."

Deborin's reaction was one of embarrassed pleasure. "It is good you have this feeling," he said. "Peoples who are different and have all the time suspicions, they do not get a friendship from the speeches of diplomats who are always having the conference. But with things of sports, and culture things, it is possible for different peoples to come more close. Is that not so?"

Bratton looked away from the netting and into the strange twinkle below Deborin's dense, black eyebrows, and tugged at the empty sleeve of his missing left arm. "It sure is."

"I believe much in this," Deborin went on. "You will remember the Olympics? It was the first time that your athletes talk with our athletes. There was much friendship, yes"

"That's right."

"And it was the same at the culture exchange when your singers and your peoples that make the jazz, they come to my country. They talk together of the things they make, and this was also much friendship. It is nice when this things happens."

Bratton gnawed on the temple of his dark glasses, and nodded.

"And you see," Deborin continued, "now you call me Mike, and this is to me a friendship. It is the sports that makes this happen, that now I am not a Russian people and you are not an American people, but we are two peoples which are friends. This gives me a feeling that is nice."

Bratton's own nice feeling glowed when his men delivered a seventh run in their half of the sixth, and there was little doubt now that Reeves could almost coast to his twenty-second win of the season. But the feeling had been glowing for weeks dating back, as Bratton thought of it now, to Bunny Beadle's shredding of *The Daily Worker* in the White Sox clubhouse. Irate and humiliated, Stepan Bukharov had stomped out that day, growling some vague threat of retaliation. But nothing of import had occurred. There had been, of course, the incident of the flag but that had amounted to but a brief unpleasantness and as far as the players were concerned it had created scarcely a ruffle.

Bratton had fully expected that the irritation which Bukharov had brought with him from Washington would inflame into an ugly boil, spewing its malevolent pus and infecting his players with enough resentment to make a shambles of their morale. But it didn't come off that way, and Bratton reasoned that it was because Bukharov now was seldom around to agitate. Perhaps because of the humiliation suffered at the hands of Beadle, and again at the hands of Miss Wiley during the flag crisis, and perhaps because of the pressure of duties at the embassy, Bukharov was spending less and less time with the team. It was true that Malsynenko, the insufferable correspondent, had slithered into the breach during Bukharov's mysterious absences, but Bratton was relieved that the players, and especially Deborin, were finally being spared Bukharov's demoralizing intrusions, his spleenish haunting of the dugout and clubhouse.

The most dramatic effect of Bukharov's withdrawl from the scene (for trips to Cuba, it was said) was that the weeks that followed had been exceptionally good ones for the White Sox. The team, riding the momentum of pulling even with the Yankees, had broken away to a spectacular fourteen-game winning streak just as the New Yorkers, plagued by an uncommon rash of injuries, went into a season-end falter.

And now the magic number was one—a Sox win or another Yankee loss—and the pennant would return to Chicago for the first time in years. Bratton's mouth was dry again, and he licked his lips and then nodded with his head toward Reeves in the pitcher's box.

"Talk about poetry in action," he said, his voice almost a croak. "Look at that guy unwind, look at the way his leg kicks up when he lets go. That's poetry."

"In what he does," Deborin said, "he is the true artist."

"We take it all today, Mike. They can't catch us now. That's going to make you a hero back in Russia, isn't it?"

"They will be very happy in my country, I am sure. I am happy, too. But I would be more happy if this very nice things happen in Chicago. It is sad, a little, that this so supreme triumph it does not happen in our stadium."

"Don't you worry about Chicago. In about half an hour all hell's going to bust loose out there."

Bratton had reached to the bench for a towel, so he did not see the ball after it left the bat. He heard the crack, followed immediately by a faint crunch and then the dirge of low moans rising from the stands, and the sickening sounds told him what he would see before he turned around.

When he reached the pitcher's box, just a pace behind the flapping white slacks of club trainer Nick Dorsey, Bratton saw Reeves writhing on his stomach, his fingers clawing into the sandlike loam on the mound. Dorsey turned him over gently until he lay on his back, the saliva making a ring of mud around his mouth, and it was as if the wind had been knocked out of him. He lay there, no one saying anything while he strained for an even breath, then he looked up at Bratton and patted his left thigh. "Right on the knee," he gasped, his face a grimace of pain. "I didn't see it coming, Horace. I never saw it."

Dorsey tucked his fingers under the elastic and lifted the pants leg and slowly pulled down the striped woollen stocking, and when he saw the bloody fragment of kneecap jutting from the skin he quickly called for the stretcher. Bratton signaled for Andre Holmes, his number one reliever, to come in from the bullpen and, head down, he followed the stretcher into the clubhouse. Standing by the trainer's table, while Dorsey gingerly fingered the wound, he was ashamed of his thoughts and appalled that all of Reeves' suffering could not brush them from his mind.

At length, Dorsey looked up. "You and I are taking a little ride to the hospital," he said, aware that his casual air was fooling no one.

Bratton, who had moved to the doorway where three or four players had come in off the bench, summoned Dorsey with a wag of his head. "Out for the series?" he whispered.

Dorsey's voice was also muted. "Out for the series?" he repeated, his lips taut. "Don't put him in the lineup next year."

On the field, the eighth inning had been rocky for reliever Holmes who had given up three runs on a walk and two hits (including a homerun), but he found his stride when Boston came up for its last turn at bat and set the Red Sox down in order. Hundreds of Boston fans, who had been rooting for Chicago to eliminate the Yankees anyway, began to scramble onto the field to get in on the hero-touching melee. But Reeves' accident had had a sobering effect on the players, throwing a damper on the elation of earlier innings, and the pennant triumph now took on a sedate aura of anticlimax. Self-conscious and almost grave, the players shook hands fleetly and then, as if by signal, they turned their backs on the screaming horde descending from the stands and half-ran through the dugout and into the clubhouse.

A woman in the locker room? Why, it was unheard of, Bratton said. Undignified!

His daughter sipping champagne with the players? *Nyet,* Deborin snorted. Improper!

But paunchy Mike Dewar, the club's publicity director and traveling secretary, was a persistent man. He had vowed that if the Sox won the pennant he would blanket every big newspaper in Europe with pictures of the event. And after years as a press agent, he swore by one maxim that nearly never failed—when in doubt, put a pretty girl in the picture.

So for days he had badgered Deborin and Bratton to break precedent, and finally they had relented. Tasia would be allowed to visit the pennant party, but for ten minutes of picture-taking only. And only after the players had pledged to mind their manners, watch their language and keep their shirts on—as Dewar put it—until after she left. The stunt was Dewar's *pièce de rèsistance* and, with an assist from the champagne he'd been sampling (to make sure it was properly chilled), it gave him a tingle.

Tasia tingled, too, but it was from the unaccustomed place she was in and the absolutely strange (and rather amusing) behavior of the players. They were as little boys let out of school for the summer, she thought, and it made her glow inside to see these grown men shed the anxiety and tenseness they had lived with for such long weeks. But they were odd ones, these Americans, when they celebrated a victory. How unusual, for example, to see a young athlete throw a shoe at the backside of such a distinguished man as Commissioner Kirk, and then—gracious!—to see the Commissioner laugh and throw it back at the young man. Such droll things they did—slapping and hugging each other, and singing (somewhat off key, she thought), and soaking towels under the faucet and flinging them across the room at just anyone. And over there, in the corner, wasn't that Jim Nelson—his picture was on that very first bubble-gum card she'd seen in Gander—pouring (of all things!) champagne on Mr. Bratton's head? How incredible. . . .

She followed Dewar as he led her through the crowded tumult of newspaper and television reporters and technicians pushing and shouting at each other. (How did they get their work done under such distracting conditions?) She stepped gingerly over the wriggling crisscross of black-rubber cables laid about the floor by the radio and television people, and it all made her think of a snake pit. And she felt a little safer when she reached her father's side.

"They are so joyous," she said, "even after the terrible accident."

"We do not tell them immediately how serious he is hurt," Deborin said. "They deserve, for a little time, to be happy, even foolish."

She wondered why the newsmen converged so much on Bunny Beadle. And Dewar, sipping contentedly, explained how Beadle had made the game's final put-out—a sizzling liner far to his right—and the play had earned him, in Reeves' absence, the winning ball. She found it intriguing to watch Beadle trying to fend off the just-one-more demands of the photographers to show the winning ball to Bratton and to Kirk and to her father and then to all of them as a group.

From behind one of the cameras came a shout: "Hey, Beadle! How about a shot of you and the Russian dame?"

"Naw, none of that stuff," Beadle shot back, tucking in the loose flaps of his shirt.

"Oh, come on!" the voice behind the camera persisted. "We got some glamour, here. Let's use it!"

"Lay off, will you?" Beadle snapped. "Get the other guys in the pictures, why don't you?"

Ever alert to anything that meant good publicity, Dewar had taken Tasia by the hand and led her to where the action was and before Beadle realized what had happened she was standing at his side, smiling at him and sometimes blinking as the bulbs flashed.

"Don't just stand there like you lost the pennant," came a shout from the back. "Put your arm around her or something."

A slight crimson flush surged to Beadle's face, and Tasia wondered if it came from shyness or irritation. She leaned toward him and said, in a low voice:

"You are angry?"

"Naw," Beadle said. "I'm not mad. It's just that they don't really need all this schmaltz. I think they're putting me on."

A portly photographer, his coat pockets bulging with flat film-holders, waddled forward, said, "You don't mind, do you, Bunny?" and slipped Tasia's arm into Beadle's.

"This has never happened to me before," Tasia said, as the picture-taking resumed. "For me it is a big experience."

"I've got news for you," Beadle said, and finally he smiled. "I don't do this every day, either."

The photographers thanked the two and turned their attention to the other players, some of whom were sitting on benches, kicking off their shoes and sipping champagne out of paper cups. The shouting was louder, now, and the jostling increased as the television crews tried to maneuver their equipment through the throng for interviews with Bratton and Deborin. Tasia and Beadle watched in amused silence, until they were suddenly aware of Malsynenko standing at their side, his watery eyes fixed on Tasia. His gray cowlick in disarray again, he looked, as usual, thoroughly worn out.

"The photographs are finished," he said to Tasia with a weary smile, "but the maker of photographs has forgotten to unjoin the arm."

Tasia was taken aback and embarrassed. "*Da!*" she said, releasing Beadle's arm. Beadle couldn't make up his mind whether Malsynenko was joshing or serious.

From his pocket, Malsynenko plucked a sheaf of yellow note paper and a pencil. "Mr. Beadle," he said, "I am preparing an article for later about the athletes of the club. I am curious about your name Bunny. It is not common this name, no?"

Beadle glanced at Tasia, shifting his feet uneasily. "What do you mean?"

"This name Bunny is not often, like Joseph, and John. I am curious because I have found it means the rabbit."

"It's not my real name. It's—"

"You have changed your name?"

"No. It's a nickname."

"A nick—?"

"A nickname. It's short for my real name. Look, what do you want to get into that for?"

"Then what is your real name, Mr. Beadle?"

Beadle looked at Tasia again, and then at his feet, and said nothing.

"I very much would like to know your name," Tasia said. "I would."

Beadle felt uncomfortable. "Well . . . it's Bunyan," he said. "When I was a kid, the other kids started calling me Bunny for short and—well, it stuck, that's all."

"Bunyan," Malsynenko repeated as he scribbled. "That is a legend man in your country, yes?"

"Yeah. He was like a hero. You know, real big."

"He was a hero, I have read, because of the great talent for speaking the lies, yes?"

Beadle began to seethe. "Look," he said, "I want to get out of these dirty clothes and—"

It was then that he felt the jarring whack between his shoulder blades and heard Dewar's exultant shout, and before he could control it a brown-stained wavelet of tobacco-juice spittle spurted from his mouth as he spoke and swashed in an arc over Malsynenko's hands and notes, slavering part of his sleeves.

Dewar, a touch tipsy and unaware of the expectoration he had caused and the drooling mess on Malsynenko, slapped Beadle again. "We made it, Bunny!" he whooped. "By God, we made it! !"

After Malsynenko reached the sink the batboy, Jerry Thiel, hurriedly brought him towels and Dewar helped him clean up. Mortified, Beadle brushed past Tasia and walked to the ice-filled tub in the center of the room.

"Now I do need a drink," he said. "That was a pretty thing for a lady to see, wasn't it?"

"You must not trouble yourself," she said. "It was an accident."

He poured the champagne slowly into the cup and offered it to her, but she declined. "Well, I suppose if you're going to chew tobacco you're going to have moments like this," he said. "I'm real sorry."

"It is nothing," she said. "Perhaps Malsynenko now will not be so curious in the future."

She watched Beadle for a few moments as he sipped. "This chewing, it makes you better when you are in the arena?"

Beadle finished the contents of the cup and dropped it on the floor. "No," he said. "It's just a filthy habit I picked up."

There was no remonstrance in her voice: "Then why do you do it?"

"Frankly, I don't know. I don't smoke, and I guess it takes the place of smoking. You know, it relaxes you a little."

"Does it not hurt the white on your teeth?"

"Well, I don't suppose it does 'em any good."

"But your teeth, they are very nice. It is sad that this chewing, it will hurt the white."

"Well, look now, let's not get carried away. They're just teeth. It's not like—"

"But no, no," Tasia exclaimed. "They are—they are beautiful, and you should keep them beautiful!"

Beadle looked away and said nothing. He was beginning to feel uneasy again. "I hate to bounce you out of this party," he said, "but the guys are itching for a shower."

Tasia smiled. "I go, now," she said.

When Beadle finally reached his hotel room, which he shared with Ken Powers, the drawling, easygoing centerfielder was sitting on the bed, snapping the locks on his bag. "Where you been?" he asked. "We leave for the airport in half an hour."

Beadle went directly to his dresser and took his shorts and underclothes out of the top drawer. "I went to the hospital to see Jim," he said.

"Dammit!" Powers said. "I clean forgot about that. How is he?"

"His knee's busted all to hell. He feels lousy."

"Why didn't you tell me you was going? I shoulda been there too."

"What am I, your keeper or something?"

"It ain't that, Bunny. But the pennant, and the party and all that, I just clean forgot."

"So I went for you. That's what the player representative's for, isn't it?"

"You don't have to get so damned touchy about it."

Beadle walked hurriedly to the clothes closet, picked up his bag, opened it on his bed and started packing. "Forget it," he said. "They're going to move him to a Chicago hospital after the operation. Go see him there."

"Operation?"

"Yeah."

"He told you?"

"Bratton did. He was there with Deborin."

Powers picked up the telephone and summoned a bell-boy for the luggage. "Well," he said, cradling the receiver, "there goes the World Series."

Beadle rolled his crumpled pajamas into a breadloaf and tossed them into the bag. "That's right," he said grimly. "His first chance to pitch the World Series. He sure gets the breaks, doesn't he?"

Powers tried to ease the tension. "Well," he said, with a forced smile, "maybe next year."

Beadle stuffed several pairs of socks into the corners of the bag. "There won't be a next year," he said. "I don't think Jim'll ever pitch again."

Powers, who had been laying on the bed with his hands behind his head, sat upright. "My God!" he said, his voice in shock. He tried to think of something to say, but couldn't.

Beadle went into the bathroom and gathered his belongings from the shelves of the medicine cabinet. He closed the cabinet door and gazed in the mirror for a moment. Then he bared his teeth and stared at them intently.

"Ken," he called out, his teeth still clenched together, "you chew, don't you?"

"Yeah."

"Does it stain your teeth?"

"Hell, I dunno. When I think of it, I take 'em out and shine 'em."

"No kidding, though. I wonder if that stuff browns them."

"I don't think it helps none. Hurry it up, will you? The boy's here for the bags."

Beadle returned to the bed, dropped his tubes and other containers into the bag and closed the lid. "Okay," he said. "All set."

The bellboy, an aging man with a limp and a glint of baseball worship in his eyes, picked up the two bags.

"They're waiting for you fellows in the bus," he said. He opened the door and started out into the doorway.

Suddenly, Beadle stopped and retrieved his bag from the bellboy's hand. "I forgot something," he said. "I'll only be a second."

He whirled around and returned to the bathroom and closed the door. Then he reopened the bag and ran his hands under the clothes until his fingers felt what they were looking for. They came out with two large plugs of chewing tobacco, wrapped in green paper and covered with cellophane.

He looked at the packages, as if debating what to do. Then he leaned over and placed them soundlessly at the bottom of the wastebasket beneath the sink.

He closed the bag again, and looked into the mirror and again he bared his teeth. Then he walked back to where Powers and the bellboy waited in the doorway. "All right," he said. "Let's go."

10

For Adelaide Wiley, the unsolicited role of confidante to Tasia was intriguing, even flattering, but it sometimes frightened her. At her age—fifty-two to herself, forty-eight to the world—it was a totally new experience and when she stopped to think of the responsibilities it involved, she caught herself rubbing her finger tips together with more vigor than was her custom.

But there was more than that to the stepup in Miss Wiley's fidgets.

It depressed her to think about it, in the loneliness of her room after work, but in the waning weeks of summer she had become dispirited over her future. For soon the disposition of Mr. Childers' estate would be at an end, and the committee of overseers appointed by Ambassador Galynin would disband. When that happened she would be, as the expression went among the ball players, at liberty.

True, she would not have financial worries, thanks to the generous provisions in Mr. Childers' will and because of a shrewd instinct for saving during her twenty-two years as his secretary. But solvency was not her concern, now. It was, as it often is for those who live alone, to be needed —as Mr. Childers had needed her, and as the interim committee disposing of his estate had needed her after his death. Now she knew that soon she would be cast adrift,

toward an inevitable isolation and away from the intoxi-
cating turmoil of the strange world of baseball into which
she had moved for too brief a time. Away, too, from the
friendly people who walked that world: Tasia, the little
girl lost who asked for her ear then stole her heart; Mike
Dewar, who made a career of being a bachelor and whose
hangovers, Miss Wiley knew, were more loneliness than
liquor; Bratton, who made a ritual of stopping by her seat
to chat whenever she attended a game; Bunny Beadle, who
had made her one of the group by dubbing her "den
mother," and even Deborin, who had remembered her
birthday—Tasia had mentioned it—with roses from Detroit
(she had nourished them until, deathly purple, they had
begun to drop). Being with these odd, impetuous people
had been such fun, and she would miss them.

Certainly she would miss moments like this one, spending her lunch hour with Tasia in the sedate, chandeliered
dining room of the Childers-Chicago Hotel, inquiring about
her childhood in Kiev or her sculpture studies at the Acad-
emy of the Arts in Moscow (discontinued on her mother's
death), or sharing her thrill over a new hat, or simply
laughing at the story of how next her father would give
his bodyguards the slip.

Now the problem was Bukharov again and Miss Wiley,
who was developing into a fairly astute counselor, found
herself limited this time to little more than sympathetic
clucks. Her bewilderment was understandable; she had
only the haziest notion of what Tasia was talking about
because Tasia herself was vague to begin with. Tasia, it
seemed, had overheard her father on the telephone with
Bukharov in Washington and seen him become disturbed
during the conversation, which had been mostly a ha-
rangue by Bukharov. He had refused to confide his mis-
givings to Tasia beyond a disquieting groan that there was
new trouble ahead from his superiors. In vain Tasia had
tried to draw him out; he had shrugged her off, muttering
that the crisis was one she would not understand.

But she had heard enough, from the remarks Deborin had been able to inject into the conversation, to speculate that the dilemma in some way involved the President of the United States and a highly placed Russian leader— quite possibly the Premier himself. As best as she could reconstruct the conversation, Bukharov was indignant because he had learned that the President, in what was plainly an underhanded propaganda move, would make a surprise appearance at Comiskey Park during the World Series. The object, as Bukharov saw it, was publicly to display his support of the National League team, thus unnerving the White Sox players and undermining their morale so that the championship would not be won by the Russian-controlled club.

"I refuse to believe it!" Miss Wiley exclaimed, pouring herself a second cup of tea. "I've never heard of such a thing."

"But that is what they were talking," Tasia said, adding that as she understood it, the President planned to do more —he would actually participate in the game. "I heard my father tell Bukharov: 'But how can they let the President throw some balls?'"

"Gracious!" said Miss Wiley. "Are you sure your father isn't pulling your leg?"

"My leg?"

"You're sure this isn't some silly joke?"

Tasia made it clear that her father was in anything but a joking mood. Indeed, he had indulged in a rare Tartar curse when Bukharov went on to promise that the United States would not get away with this vile capitalistic chicanery. It cried out, Bukharov insisted, for equal representation by a Soviet statesman and the Kremlin had already been alerted.

"Dear me," Miss Wiley said, "whatever would the President be doing at a baseball game? It seems like a dreadful waste of time."

"I do not know," Tasia said. "My father, he does not know also. But he is angry because this will cause much trouble. Also he is very sad for to tell the players."

Miss Wiley idly stirred her tea, and then her memory. "You know," she said, "maybe Bukharov is right. I remember seeing a newsreel on television about the President doing something at a ball game."

"Yes?"

"He was looking at the ball, as if he was examining the seams. But that doesn't make sense, does it? I'm sure the ball was sewn properly."

"I do not know. . . ."

"Then, I remember, he threw the ball at some players, and he was laughing. And then he threw another one, and another one, and a lot of photographers were running around taking pictures. It must have been a ceremony of some sort. Oh, dear! I do wish I knew more about baseball!"

Tasia was forlorn because she knew that whatever Bukharov had proposed as retaliation, her father was reluctant to it and there was no doubt that it would eventually embarrass him in front of the players. "I wish it too," she said. "Also I wish we should tell somebody so they will know my father this is not his fault."

"Yes, we should. Perhaps we should talk to Bratton."

Tasia had been folding and unfolding her napkin until the original creases were lost. She examined her hands in silence, then said: "Do you think better than Mr. Bratton I should tell this to Bunny Beadle? He is the representative of the players."

Miss Wiley gazed into her empty cup and then, as if she had found something at the bottom she had been looking for, a small smile began to take form on her lips but she quickly concealed it with the back of her hand. "You're right," she said finally. "I think you should see him as soon as possible."

The prospect of another confrontation with Stepan Bukharov had been utterly distasteful to Bunny Beadle, and he had vowed to himself that he would have nothing to do with Tasia's suggestion. Why should he stick his nose into a matter that belonged to high international diplomacy? He was, after all, only a ball player and it would be the height of arrogance for him to try to dissuade a Soviet official from a project that apparently involved the President of the United States and, as threatened, the top dog in Russia. Even if it was a fool scheme.

And a fool scheme it was, he had told Tasia at dinner the night before. How naïve could she be, for instance, to imagine that the President of the United States would take part in a ball game in order, as she had put it, to bring about the collapse of her father's team? It was un-American. It was un-presidential. And on top of all that it was absolutely unbelievable.

Tasia had relaxed, somewhat, after Beadle had explained why the President would be attending the first game of the World Series to begin with: Traditionally, the President appeared on opening day in the spring at D.C. Stadium in Washington to toss out the first ball and get the season under way. But illness in April had interrupted the custom and the President had promised to make up for the disappointment by showing up at World Series time. The fact that it was only a brief ceremony and had nothing to do with the Chief Executive's team preference, if any, gave Tasia a measure of relief, but it did not dispel her fears of Bukharov's intentions and the concern she had for what his suspicious plans would do to her father's image.

Yet as much as he felt for Tasia's anxiety, Beadle was resolute; he could not inject himself into what surely would become an international incident. Even if he could interfere in his capacity of player representative he would be risking the wrath of the State Department. No. He was truly sorry, he understood her feelings but the angles on this one were just too messy to fool around with.

Imagine, he thought, groping under the bed for his loafers, Russia's number one man throwing a baseball in an American ball park. It made no sense! Then he remembered the sight of the number one man removing a shoe during a United Nations meeting and slapping it on his desk, and he wondered. . . . Still, for him, Bunny Beadle, to move into such a silly situation as Tasia had outlined. . . . Why, it was impossible. It was insane.

And now, as he sat staring through the thick glasses into Bukharov's eyes, he wondered why he had gotten himself into such an insane, impossible situation. He followed Bukharov's stern gaze as it fixed first on his outrageously orange sports shirt, open at the collar, then on his cream-colored slacks and finally on his gray suede loafers. He could tell by the tilt of Bukharov's nose and the semblance of a sneer on his mouth that the Russian was offended by his attire. Beadle was aware that he had hardly the elegance expected of one who had come to call on the First Secretary to the Russian Embassy. But this was his way of returning the snub, for Bukharov had insisted that if Beadle had to talk to him it would be downstairs in the hotel lobby, and not in his hotel room. And where Beadle had expected a private chat, Bukharov had shown up in the lobby with Malsynenko whom Beadle now considered more a press agent for the embassy than a newspaper correspondent.

Beadle pulled in his long legs—at six feet four he was the tallest player on the team—and clasped his hands around his knees. "So you won't drop the idea?" he said, looking first at Bukharov and then at Malsynenko.

"Certainly I shall not!" Bukharov growled, launching into a censure of the impertinence of Americans who meddled in affairs that did not concern them. But Beadle was not listening. His thoughts were on Tasia and how she had looked at dinner the night before. She had again worn the white beret tilted fetchingly to one side, and he had come very near telling her that he thought it stunning. Good heavens, was he starting to fall for this funny little girl?

". . . and for the glory of the Union of Soviet Socialist Republics," Bukharov was saying.

"Of course," Beadle said, idly patting the bristle-like top of his crewcut. No, he couldn't be falling for her. A Commie dame? It was just that a fellow got to notice a girl more if she was from another country, and she had an accent and she was kind of helpless.

". . . if our Premier comes to the United States," Bukharov droned on.

"I don't think you'll get your Premier here," Beadle said. Suddenly he felt a strange courage, and it seemed to make him giddy.

"I have—how do you say it?—a alternate plan," Bukharov said, adjusting his plump backside to the sinking couch. "Ambassador Leonid Galynin, he is the personal representative of our Premier in this country. He will throw, in the absence of the Premier, the ball."

Beadle had an immediate picture of Galynin blinking through his pince-nez. "Wouldn't it be something," he said, trying hard not to smile, "if he beaned somebody and started a riot."

"Beaned?" Bukharov said, adding another ripple to his frown.

"Never mind," Beadle said, his thoughts elsewhere again. That was it, he was sure. This was why he had talked himself into tangling with Bukharov. The girl was among strange people, lost and afraid, and she had to turn to someone for help.

Still, there were others she could have turned to. But she had turned to him.

". . . and anything else would be an insult to my country," Bukharov was saying.

Beadle watched as a slender man with a fledgy red beard and a white card pinned to his lapel stepped briskly out of the elevator, paused to glance at his watch, then headed for the coffee shop. When, he wondered, had this strange feeling started? Not last night at dinner, because he remembered the first time he had been intrigued by the little white hat and the way it sat askew on her head, and he remembered wondering what kept it from slipping off. It was the night the others had left him alone with her at the nightclub table as they danced, when the wisps of black hair had bounced on her cheeks as she cocked her head from side to side, and he had flattened the drunk and the warm tingle had coursed into his arms and legs and even—he was sure—into his ears. Only once had he felt this tingle before, and that had been the night in Cleveland when he had walloped his first (and only) Major League grand-slam homerun. And once since he had felt it: That had been the other day in Boston, the day of the pennant. But it was not the pennant that had done it. It was the touch of her arm thrust into his.

". . . and I am curious, Mr. Beadle," Bukharov was saying, "on who sent you to discuss with me."

A middle-aged man, grinning self-consciously, stopped by Beadle's chair with his son, and the boy, serious and a little afraid, presented a crumpled piece of paper and a pencil and as he signed his name Beadle was abruptly jolted by the thought that love—was it really that?—could come into the life of a twenty-six-year-old man with such suddenness.

Yet had it really been sudden? He remembered now the little things, or what seemed to have been little things at the time. . . . The strange tempest somewhere in his chest when he had first seen her on the loading ramp at the airport, her mouth open and laughing as she hugged Deborin's arm . . . the curious elation on learning that she was not his wife . . . the many times he had glanced casually from second base to where she usually sat during the games, and the distress no one suspected when her chair was vacant . . . the maddening frustration that lavender eyes—the first he had ever seen—and such svelte loveliness could reside in the body of a Communist.

Bukharov, arms crossed, was drumming his fingers on his elbows. "I ask," he rumbled, "who sent you. Commissar Deborin?"

"None of your damned business," Beadle snapped, his cockiness back.

"His daughter, no doubt," Malsynenko said, breaking the silence he had kept since arriving in the lobby.

"So why do you ask?" Beadle said.

"We know you have been seeing her," Bukharov said.

"I know you know," Beadle said. "And you want to know something else? I couldn't care less what you know."

Bukharov sucked in his breath, and it made a tinny, whistling sound. "I could arrange that she does not see you—"

"Listen, jerk," Beadle broke in, "you're not in Russia now! So don't give me that baloney."

Bukharov started up again. "I could arrange that she does not see you, but this is not necessary. Because soon she will not see you forever. Soon, when the tournament is concluded, she will be sent home with her father. And this I tell you, Mr. Beadle—she will come again never to this country!"

Beadle was taken aback but he tried valiantly not to show it. "That how you guys operate? It's great, that power over human beings, isn't it?"

He stood up, arms akimbo. "But I'm not surprised," he said, glowering at Bukharov who was trying to pull himself out of the sunken softness of the couch, "because that's about your speed—picking on a girl. A defenseless girl! You wouldn't dare push a man around, would you, you gutless Commie!"

Bukharov finally rose to a standing position, and now he was breathing hard. "In the contrary, Mr. Beadle," he rasped. "I do not retreat of pushing a man. I will push you!

I will push you soon out of the club which my country owns!"

Again Beadle was bewildered. "Oh, you will, will you?" he said, stalling for thought.

A redness rose to Bukharov's face. "Yes," he said. "I did not wish to announce it now, but you have much insolence and you are a barbarian, so I tell you now the news. After the tournament, you will not be any more a member of the White Sox organization. You will be dismissed!"

"Yeah? By who?"

"I shall dismiss you. And I shall dismiss also all your colleagues! I have the authority now to do this thing."

Beadle grunted a nervous laugh. "So you're going to fire us all? Great! Maybe you'll play second base next year. And how about your pal, here, for pitcher?"

"Laugh now!" Bukharov said, wagging his finger in Beadle's face. "There will be a Soviet club next year, but you and your bourgeois friends will not be on it."

Beadle hitched his slacks and his breath was on Bukharov's eyeballs. "I can hardly wait," he sneered.

Malsynenko rose and placed a restraining hand on Bukharov's arm. "It is better not to tell him more," he said softly.

Bukharov ignored him. "Soon," he said, "very soon you will see a large surprise, Mr. Beadle. In my country we have a saying: 'He who finds a well is wise to retain the shovel.'"

Beadle noticed that a few stragglers in the lobby were staring at the argument, and he forced himself to keep his voice low. "And in my country," he said, "we have a saying, too. Drop dead!"

He turned and took long strides across the lobby with his head down. At the newsstand he tossed a dime on the glass counter, picked a *Chicago Sun-Times* from the top of the pile and walked away without waiting for his change, turning immediately to the sports section at the back of the paper. In the taxi he leaned back, reading hurriedly, and he felt good again, all the anger gone from him for now. The

St. Louis Cardinals had won their afternoon game in Pitts-
burgh, gasping into a first-place tie and clinching a playoff
with the Los Angeles Dodgers for the National League
Pennant. This was wonderful, a dream he had had for years.
Now if the Cards could just knock over the Dodgers, he
would get to play in a World Series in his hometown.

He flipped the paper back to the front page and instinc-
tively his right foot darted to a brake that was not there.
"Turn this thing around," he told the driver, "and go back
to the hotel."

He hummed impatiently into the house phone while the
operator rang Tasia's room, and he noticed his hands had
become moist. When she answered, he said: "This is Bunny.
I'm downstairs. The dragon's dead."

"The dragon? I—"

"Never mind. I'm going into the bar and if you'll come
down and meet me there I'll lie about your age and they'll
let you in." He heard her deep-throated giggle and savored
it and then looked around furtively, a little astounded to
find himself feeling passionate on a telephone.

At the entrance to the dimly lit bar, Tasia stood uncer-
tainly, scanning the tables—it was so seldom she saw him
in street clothes—and then she recognized the outline of the
huge shoulders beneath the orange shirt just as they turned
toward her. Beadle stood as she reached his table and he
saw why she had taken so long to come down. She was
wearing the gray sheath again, the one with the narrow
belt that he had once said he liked on her, and now the
place no longer seemed dimly lit for little lights went on
around him though he could not see them. It pleased him
that because he was having beer she ordered a bottle, too,
and as she sipped he stared at the flashes of lavender between her long lashes and the view was so much nicer than
from second base.

She put down her glass and smiled. "Now you will tell
me about the dragon, yes?"

He pushed his bottle to the side and dropped his arms

on the table. "Tasia," he said, and she was quick to catch what looked like mischief in his brown eyes, "what would you say if I told you the problem is solved? I mean about Bukharov and getting the Premier down here and all that stuff?"

Tasia brought her hands together, as if she were going to clap them. "I would say good, good!" she exclaimed. "Very much good!"

"It'd make you happy?"

"Oh, so much happy I could—I could—"

"You could kiss me?"

Tasia lifted her glass, as something to hide her face. "Oh, Bunny," she said in a flustered whisper. "I—you are . . . Yes!"

"Then you're stuck with it. Because it all happened."

Tasia was sure the others at nearby tables were listening. "But Bunny," she stammered. "I cannot . . . You . . . But not here!"

Gently he took the glass away from her and then he leaned over and kissed the back of her hand. And then he released her hand and they looked into each other's eyes for a long, silent moment.

"I am very much happy," she said at last. "You must tell me please what happened."

She watched the funny, crooked smile twitch to life on his mouth as his arm reached underneath his chair and came back with the paper. He placed it on the table where her glass had been. She read the large black headline.

PRESIDENT TO VISIT WEST BERLIN

"He leaves next week," Beadle explained as she frowned over the front page. "He'll be in Europe a month, so he won't be here to throw that first ball. And that takes care of Comrade Bukharov."

Tasia looked up from the paper and she was smiling again. "Oh, Bunny," she said. "It was not you who did this. You cheat me!"

"I didn't say I'd done it. I just said it happened. So I only cheated a little."

Slowly, fondly she rubbed the back of her hand, where he had kissed it. "I . . . I am happy," she said, "that you cheat me."

The waiter saw their empty glasses and started toward them but when he came near to their table he veered and went to another. It would be best to come back later, he thought.

11

For Mikhail Deborin, it was a relief to be rid of a wretched habit.

Over the years as an official of high party function in Russia, he had conditioned himself to think ahead. Projection was a characteristic of the Politburo, and since the trait seeped down to all levels of government the functionary who wanted to hold onto his job weaned on it with what sounded to the untrained ear like contented gurgles. As Deputy Chairman of the Central Council of the All-Union Committee on Sports and Culture, Deborin had found himself, like other deputy chairmen, living a great deal of the time in a futuristic void bounded on all sides by grandiosely impossible five-year plans—and some of longer duration. For the most part, his career had been one of long-range planning and such was the preoccupation with tomorrow that it frequently made a shambles of today, and in time he had found it appropriate to replace the memo pad on his desk with a five-year calendar.

But Horace Bratton had done much to temper his obsession, at least for a time. Calm and seldom ruffled, the veteran manager had quickly impressed him with his insistence on worrying for the moment only, and by the time Deborin had learned to calculate an earned-run average he had come to admire Bratton's design for serenity: "I play each game as it comes, one at a time and to hell with tomorrow until tomorrow."

This frame of mind had sustained Deborin during the unnerving early weeks, when public reaction to the new "chairman" of the Chicago White Sox bounced between disdain and approval. As the gap between the Yankees and Sox began to close, the excitement of the race drove almost everything else from his thoughts, so that when pennant fever struck the team he had closed his mind to all things except the day-to-day ordeal of each game as it came.

Then came the pennant, and with it an emotional letdown prolonged by the lack of suspense in the games remaining for the Sox to play. Thus, during the rain-swept week that it took the Dodgers to keep the National League pennant from going to St. Louis, a series which put the Sox in layoff, Deborin found plenty of time for matters he had earlier nudged aside under the sustained pressure of the pennant race.

There was, foremost, his relationship with the embassy in Washington which had very nearly fallen into disrepair. It distressed him that a breach had come between him and Ambassador Galynin, because he had taken a liking to him from the day the tall, smiling diplomat had met the Deborin plane in New York. Galynin had gone to much effort to make sure that Deborin and Tasia were comfortable while in the United States, and had insisted on unlimited expense toward a gracious style of living for the two of them (though Deborin had been more embarrassed than flattered when Galynin supplied him with bodyguards, he suffered them out of regard for the Ambassador's feelings).

The coolness began to develop, he remembered, after he asked Bukharov, at Bratton's urging, to watch the game from the stands instead of from the dugout. Expectedly, Bukharov ignored the request and soon after *The Daily Worker* incident in the clubhouse Deborin noticed a change in Galynin's attitude, even in his personality. The Ambassador no longer flew in to see a Chicago game as he occasionally did in earlier, happier days when his work allowed it. He even ceased coming to the games that the Sox played in Washington. He seldom telephoned Deborin, now, to inquire about the team's welfare, and when he did call his voice was stern and it was usually to register his concern over something Deborin had done (or not done, as in the controversy over the flag). Even after what Deborin considered his finest moment, a pennant for the Kremlin, there was not so much as a telegram from the embassy.

Deborin knew very well that it was Bukharov who was casting the dark shadow. Not too subtly, Bukharov had tried early in the season to use the team for propaganda and other purposes, and while Deborin found Bukharov's zeal understandable he could not share it to the point of collaborating with him. He had, after all, been sent to America to take command of an organization and his task was to lead it to success. To do this, it was necessary that he concentrate solely on the sport, and since the sport had been foreign to him to begin with, it was not right that he should become involved politically. Even if it were right, he felt, cooperation with Bukharov would be extremely difficult because the First Secretary looked on the team as a Russian property while he regarded it as a family of athletes.

In addition, Deborin had begun to feel some concern for what these complications could add to at home. Not that he was in fear; he had done his duty, and when a man does his duty there should be no reason for fear. But the fact remained that his conduct (the word Bukharov had once used, derisively) could be open to whatever interpretation Bukharov chose to give it. And while it was true that Bukharov, as First Secretary to the embassy, was a good many rungs beneath Deborin in the hierarchy of the government, it was also true that when he spoke and acted in this country he spoke and acted for the Ambassador—and the Ambassador was the direct representative of the Soviet government.

As his thoughts dwelt more and more, those recent days,

on his impending return home, Deborin felt them twinge with bittersweet emotion: It would be nice to go home again for a vacation for there was so much he missed. Of course, it was good that Tasia had been with him, but as strong as their love was for each other it could never be enough to dispel the haze of loneliness that closed in on him when he entered his hotel room at night and stood at the window, and gazed at the vast solitude of Lake Michigan below, and listened to its own restless murmur.

It was on nights such as these that he would see Nadezhda before him again and remember, with a fondness that hurt, how strongly and proudly she had loved him. It was then he would try to hold fast, almost in desperation, to the pictures that were beginning to fade, treasuring the times of her childlike delight in the simplest of things. He could almost feel her hand clasping his as it did long ago in Kiev when they walked to the banks of the Dnieper at sunset to watch the barges slip silently past the city. He could almost feel again the warmth of her body beneath the blanket as their rented troika slid along a snowy trail to a nowhere together. And always he would come back to the day at the health resort in Sochi when she promised to become strong again for him, even though Dr. Kvatoff at the clinic warned that she had the heart of a bird. And as they stood on the promenade each threw a kopeck into the Black Sea, and both laughed into the wind as it moaned above the breakers because he told her that since she had the heart of a bird she would henceforth be his little *soloveii*, his little nightingale. Afterward, they moved to the tables on the promenade and watched the older vacationers at chess, before taking the sulphur baths. And at dinner, over the *shashlik* she loved so much, she told him that this had been the happiest day of her life.

But he protested. "It was just an ordinary day. Were there not other happy days?"

"Yes. There was yesterday. It was the second happiest day."

They smiled into each other's eyes, remembering the times past, as she said, "All the days were good, and each was better than the one before."

And that night, after receiving his love, she whispered: "If I am a wounded bird, Mikhail, then you must always hold me in your hands."

"I will always hold you in my hands."

And in the morning he turned to her again but the warmth had gone from her body and there was only a cold stillness on her, and his hands were empty.

As he stood at his window, the nights during the layoff, pondering the return to his land, he thought often of what he would bring back with him. For as remembrance of home had come with him here, some memories of here would go with him home. Mostly he would bring the little surprises from those moments when he had discovered America, in his own way, in the cities where baseball had brought him so often. The unexpected things he had come upon were not the things he had read about in the thick books Tasia had packed in the trunk before they left Moscow. Nor had he read them in the articles written for magazines at home by the wives of diplomats who had come here before him. Nor were they the things that Bukharov and Malsynenko grumbled about during those long talk sessions that robbed him of his nights.

What was it they had told him about the Americans—effete and reeking of lotion, made soft by their search for pleasure and not at all like the hardy stock of Europe? But would he forget the wonder of that wet afternoon in Cleveland, when sodden skies had rained out the game and he had whiled the time walking by the twisty Cuyahoga River as the steelworkers spilled out of the immense mills toward their homes in The Flats? In less than an hour, as he stepped away from the swinging lunch pails, he had been astonished to catch the mumbling and the laughter and the cursing in accents that were Polish and Yugoslavian and German and Italian and Hungarian and Lithuanian and—

yes, the fleeting murmur of the two older men that was distinctly Russian. This was Cleveland, and these were Americans?

"They have no individuality," Malsynenko had written in one of his dispatches. "They look alike and dress alike and think alike." If only Malsynenko could have been with him the Sunday morning in Minneapolis when he had strolled past the open doors of the church (it was Our Lady of Lourdes, he remembered) and the words of the sermon had come into the street in French.

So many things to bring wonder. The National Gallery in Washington, where he waited in line with the hundreds who had queued up for the exhibition of Byzantine art. Were these the frustrated civil servants who drank too much that the Ambassador had told him about? . . . Kansas City where he saw, as he was told he would see, the clusters of billboards that sullied the face of the community, but where he had gone behind the vulgarity to find the beauty of its boulevards . . . Boston, the city of the tilted, intolerant nose—strange that it should be the first to unbend and ask him to address one of its service clubs . . . And how comprehend the calumny that Americans were loud and boorish when one found in Baltimore laws that forbade the mowing of lawns on Sunday and ended baseball games before midnight so citizens could sleep undisturbed?

And he remembered his expectations of Los Angeles as a city of sin and swimming pools, and finding it a city of sun and swimming pools and wishing that the sun would tarry as long in Kiev so that he, too, might walk from his bed in the morning to a bath and an orange in the yard . . . The caution that the slums of Detroit and the cacophony of its traffic would offend him, but cherishing the city that refused to let his beloved Bolshoi Ballet leave at the end of its American tour (and learning that American attendance at symphony concerts was larger than that at baseball parks).

Finally, Chicago and New York—Chicago and a pair of

bodyguards to fend off scowling gangsters with guns, when the only intruders to hem him in were laughing boys with pens. And New York, where he had expected faceless, nameless mole-like creatures scurrying in and out of the holes in the canyons. But all they were, really, were immigrants from the cities he had come to know and from the smaller places between.

He liked New York. He liked it very much, despite the dreadful impression it made on him the first day and night. That was after the Russian delegation drove him to the hotel, and Mike Dewar suggested a visit to the Empire State Building (no), or to the home of the United Nations (no), or to Yankee Stadium (no). He wanted to see Times Square, and so the two of them set out that afternoon as the searing, smirking sun dropped its little hell on the baked pavement, and he remembered that it bounced into his face and felt like a handful of sand flung into his eyes.

And they pushed and elbowed into what Dewar described as the biggest, noisiest, tawdriest continuous show in America—a glob of gaudy palaces and smelly holes-in-the-wall screaming for his favor above the harsh swell of feet dragging on concrete, tinkling cash registers and the vulgar whelps of doorway pitchmen. On almost every block a walk-up dance place: ENJOY YOURSELF! the signs cried. DANCE WITH BEAUTIFUL GIRLS! And below the signs, a photo gallery of tired, dull-eyed women trying to hide time under mawkish make-up. Here and there a movie house with so many exclamation points on the marquee: *"A Girl Who Goes from Lover to Lover!!" "Lusty!!!" "Racy!!!"* And he remembered the man and the woman and their two small daughters reading the sordid promise, and the man tugging at his daughters to move along . . . Gift shops galore where he could buy almost anything—a tie with his name on it; life-size figures in cardboard of busty women with fixed smiles ("Souvenir Of New York"); phonograph albums on sidewalk counters (stags, Dewar called them) with nudes cavorting on the covers, and cards that said: *Help Stamp*

Out Cadillacs! . . . Signs in the windows: COMPLETE AS-
SORTMENT OF SUNGLASSES, KNIVES, GUNS . . . Everywhere
the blare of voices over scratchy loudspeakers urging him to
come out of the heat and into the twilit alcoves . . . The
voices of spielers drowning out, and in turn being drowned
out by raucous records hurtling the monotonous beat of
rock and roll into the humid air . . . The sacrilegious legend
of "MUSEUM" on a loft where he could examine shrunken
heads and instruments of torture, and applaud the perform-
ing fleas . . . And spitting through the pandemonium, the
crack and whine of rifles from playlands and funlands and,
descending from above, where the massive mouth blew
rings of smoke, the pungent odor of corned beef and pickle,
and through it all the murmur of the crowds rising into the
oppressive air until all of it reminded him of the forbidden
revels of the gypsy caravans he had seen as a boy in Boris-
pol.

"What brings here these people?" he asked Dewar, awed
and unbelieving.

"People are looking for other people," Dewar said. "It's
lonely in New York when you're alone."

And later, the sound of talk still welling in his ears, he
stood at the open window of the hotel room at three o'clock
in the morning and wondered why the darkness did not silence the babble of the city below. In pairs and in clusters,
on corners and loping along the sidewalks, the people of
New York still talked—loudly and incessantly . . . A few
doors down the hall, he caught the rumble of voices, low
and serious and then loud with laughter . . . Nearby, an
elevator clanked open its doors, threw out a torrent of
jumbled words, then plunged down the well in mid-sen-
tence . . . In the next room, the ring of the telephone, and
he set aside his guilt and listened to the man padding hurriedly to the jangle ("Los Angeles? Yeah, put him on").
And the talk went on. Inside, Outside. On the street below,
cars stopped and cars started. Doors ground open; doors
slammed shut . . . The ricochet of blinking lights from the

signs to the neon glow in the sky that talked, talked, talked to the people of chewing gum and beer and places of pleasure. On the corner below a man and a woman, their faces on the glass, peering into a shop window and talking. A truck roaring to a halt and the men stepping out on each side, talking . . . It was three o'clock in the morning in New York and it was as if there were no night.

Many times since he had stood at windows when it seemed there was no night, and remembered what Mike Dewar had said about people looking for other people when they were alone. But all these thoughts were before, when he had had time for them.

They were not now, for now he was not alone. Now he was not looking for people.

Now he was in Comiskey Park in Chicago again, standing at home plate with Horace Bratton nearby, and on all sides he looked up at people—more than fifty-one thousand people assembled for the first game of the World Series between the Chicago White Sox and the Los Angeles Dodgers. And a hush fell on the multitude when the voice, as if from an echoing cavern, rumbled into the October wind: "Ladies and gentlemen . . . Our National Anthem."

They stood, and as they sang Bratton suddenly was startled by the rasp and croak near the plate and he marveled that stocky Len Hilts, he of the tin ear who never sang and the most feared umpire in the major leagues, had finally deferred to offer his snarling voice to the anthem. He turned discreetly to watch tradition being broken, only to discover that the odd sounds were coming not from Hilts but from Deborin. He turned away quickly so as not to disturb the strange sight of the Commissar, still in black shirt and tie and still wearing only the pants of his uniform loosely, the leggings flapping in the breeze. He gritted his teeth when Deborin sang out the words "or the rumpots we wash," and it was only with great difficulty that he restrained a panicky giggle when Deborin, the proud shine on his black shoes obliterated by dust, intoned the line, "the bums burping in there." But it was simply more than Bratton's discipline could cope with when Deborin, the yellow garters tight around his exposed calves, managed to make "strangled banana" out of "spangled banner." Bratton thrust out his chin and fisted his hands and, staring unflinchingly at the Stars and Stripes, hoped the tears forming at the corners of his eyes would pass for patriotism rather than the glandular ooze of suppressed laughter.

Back in the dugout he tried hard to concentrate on the Dodger lineup in his score-book, but he had to give in to curiosity. "That was something, you singing the anthem," he said. "I didn't expect it."

Deborin pulled a large white handkerchief from his back pocket and slapped at the dust on his shoes. "When the masses sing, not to join is much difficult," he smiled.

"Where did you learn it?"

"On the cinema that is late."

"The what?"

"The cinema that is late. On the television."

"You mean the late show, the movie?"

"Yes, the late show. I do not like to enter the bed early and I much enjoy to observe the ancient films on your television. And always, at the conclusion, there is your anthem, and so I have learned it. But some words I do not understand."

"I know what you mean. But you're fine on the melody. That's pretty good for a foreigner, catching on so fast to an American tune."

Deborin tucked the soiled handkerchief into his pocket, and his tone was frisky. "My dear Horace," he said, "as a boy I whistle this melody when I walk to the school. It is as American as—as I am."

"You're kidding!"

"It does not even belong to you. It is an old drinking song of the English."

"Oh, come on, now! English?"

"*Da*. It is a composition of the century number eighteen."

"I'll be damned!" Bratton said, looking up in time to see his lead-off man, left-fielder Clelio Pangonini, wince at a called third strike. "I'll be damned," he said again, finding it bizarre that his thoughts should stray to an eighteenth-century drinking song at the start of the most exhilarating afternoon of his life.

The thoughts were bizarre, too, in the team box between third base and home plate which was occupied by Ambassador Leonid Galynin; his First Secretary, Bukharov; Fedor Malsynenko, the correspondent, and Leon Sobolev, the chief delegate to the United Nations who was making his first visit to Chicago.

Behind them, their chairs moved as far back as they would go to the rear of the box, sat Tasia and Miss Wiley, each with a pencil and score card given them by Mike Dewar which neither planned to use. Miss Wiley had angrily given up keeping score months before, the day that first baseman Glen Leslie, who had a peculiar talent for batting into the dirt, had grounded out four successive times. "He hit the ball hard, a good smack each time," she had protested to Dewar, "and the papers said he didn't get a hit!"

As often happens at the start of a World Series, first-game jitters tightened up most of the players and the only play to bring the crowd to its feet in the first three innings was a mighty blast by Ken Powers which Dodger outfielder Dave Keefe snared by heaving his body into the left-field fence. But if there was monotony in the park, Miss Wiley was blissfully unaware of it, so engrossed had she become in Tasia's concern over the watch kept on her movements by the two Russian bodyguards. "Everywhere I go, they follow," Tasia complained. "Even now, they are here."

"In the park? Watching us?" Miss Wiley exclaimed, and the furtive thought that foreign spies had her in their gaze gave her a vicarious thrill.

"They are here."

Miss Wiley scanned the stands and it seemed that the

dozens of binoculars in the distance were aimed directly at her and Tasia, and before she could stop it a casual, nonchalant smile parted her lips slightly, and her hand went up and patted down the grayish wisps of hair. She wasn't sure if it was the autumn chill slipping in over the bleachers, but she suddenly felt a small shiver, and she enjoyed it.

And on the pitcher's mound the Dodgers' fast-ball terror, Ev Kiedaisch, cursed the unspeakable slobs who had muffed the easy double play, and he was in serious straits for the old soreness had returned to his arm.

"Even from home," Tasia said, "they wish to know all that I do. Again today the letter from Grigoriy said that I should come home."

"Tasia," Miss Wiley said, "how long have you known Grigoriy?"

"It was one year when I left. Now he writes for the journals, and he has been sent to Kharkov."

"Do you like him?"

"He is a good man, but always he writes angry. All the time he tells the people they must work harder, to make better the production in the factories of tractors and the other places of work. It is never a happy writing."

"He sounds a little boring," Miss Wiley sniffed.

Tasia laughed. "In the letter today is the article by him in *Trud*. He tells the farmers that for the glory of the fatherland they must make better the quota in the litter of pigs. Is this to you interesting, in a letter from the gentleman friend?"

"Dear me," Miss Wiley smiled, "I wish I got letters, any letters, from gentlemen. I do believe I'd even settle for pig litters, so long as some man wrote me."

In the shower stall, Kiedaisch held his aching arm under the stream of hot water. He had given up two runs on a walk and two hits, and his World Series start was a disaster. He ran out, dripping, and turned up the volume of the radio on the rubbing table, and ran back into the splash.

With her father's team ahead two to nothing, some of the

tenseness left Tasia and she pointed to Bukharov and Malsynenko in front of her and talked of the somber plans they were making for her.

"Bunny said Bukharov he wants that I go away," she said. "But I know this for a long time. I know Malsynenko tells to him all the things that I do, and even Grigoriy writes to me from Kharkov of the things I do here, and all of them together they make the plot to send me away."

"And you don't want to leave?"

"I wish to stay because my father he must stay, after the vacation, and he will need me."

"Is that the only reason?"

"Well . . ."

Miss Wiley pointed to the infield and then, smiling, patted Tasia's hand. "I see another reason," she said. "It's over there at second base."

Tasia's shy laugh was drowned out by the moan that rose from the seats around them as Jenk Simms, who had vowed to win the first one for the side-lined Jim Reeves, gave up his first walk of the day to load the bases for the Dodgers. The next batter sent a long, lazy fly to deep right and the runner on third made it home with time to spare, and in the seventh inning the Dodgers had pushed across their first run of the Series.

"Bunny is very nice," Tasia said, "and he has much surprise in his heart."

Throughout the eighth inning she talked of their movie dates and dinners in quiet places together, and how Beadle went to such pains to make himself the rough, tough, swaggering, no-sentiment, paid-to-win bruiser who would spike his own sister if she tried to steal second. But her intuition had seen through the pretense, and into the gentleness of his nature and his concern for those near him. She spoke emotionally of their recent visit to St. Louis where Beadle had driven her and Deborin to meet his father's brother, Uncle Mac, who had taken him as his own when, as a boy, he had lost both parents in an auto accident. A widower now, and slowed down by a stroke, Uncle Mac held court as a hero, since he was kin to a hero, in a convalescent home that was, Tasia said, as nice as her hotel.

"To Bunny," she went on, "his uncle is as a king, and Father said this was a thing of goodness in the heart, and a thing not often."

Now the sun dipped to leave the world for the day, and the shadows lengthened from the infield into the grass. It was the last of the ninth and the thousands, sensing a Sox victory, erupted into hoarse roars on every pitch and Simms, telling himself that he was not tiring, tried not to hear them as they screamed at him to hold on.

Miss Wiley stood up to adjust the cushion that had begun to slip off the seat. "It's terribly personal, Tasia," she said, "but I simply must ask you. Do you love him?"

"I feel that I . . . In my heart there—yes, I love him . . ."

There were no more shivers stabbing into the box and Miss Wiley felt a surge of warmth inside, and the tips of her fingers were rubbing together again.

"When did you know that you loved him?"

"The time, in the hotel, when he put on me a kiss."

The cushion began to slide sideways again but Miss Wiley didn't care. "He did?"

Now the Dodgers had a man on first again, and Simms looked at him a last time before turning away from the mound and walking back to the dugout with Bratton. "Look," Tasia cried, "we make the substitution of the pitcher!"

"Never mind that," Miss Wiley trilled. "Tell me more! Tell me more!"

Andre Holmes, the "Old Reliable" from the White Sox bullpen, arched his back and leaned low to the ground as he threw his warmup pitches with methodical swiftness, like an axman chopping a tree. Deborin, shags of silvery hair loose in the wind, stood near the third-base line, watching him in silence.

"He put on my hand a kiss," Tasia said. "He is more shy, you see, than he wishes the people to know."

"On the hand," Miss Wiley said. "Isn't that wonderful! Isn't it romantic?"

She watched Deborin kick once into the dirt and re-enter the dugout. "Bunny and your father get along well now, don't they?" she asked.

"Yes," Tasia said. "At the beginning, Bunny did not like him. I know this. But some things happen, and he said to me why he likes him."

"Because of you?" Miss Wiley said, no longer concealing her bliss.

"No. Because what Father he said to Bukharov at the angry meeting, the meeting of Bukharov to put our flag more high in the arena than the American flag. Father said he made in himself concern only for one flag, the flag that is called the pennant." Tasia laughed, remembering. "Bunny was in much joy, and he said to me: 'Tasia, your old man is hokay with me.'"

Holmes was a left-hander, assigned to play the percentage when the Dodgers sent in their pinch-hitter, Red Durham, a gigantic switch-hitter who went after outside pitches while taking a full stride forward with his body in swinging motion. Holmes leaned over, his gloved hand on his knee, and stared long at the plate.

Propped up in the hospital bed, his bandaged leg in a pulley, Jim Reeves kept his eyes on the television screen like a man hypnotized, ignoring the nurses and the lip-biting intern crowding his doorway. "He's got to keep it tight inside and low," he said, like a man talking to himself. "Tight inside and low."

The park was almost in silence now, and Tasia toyed with the knot on the pink silk scarf beneath her chin. "And so I said to him: 'Bunny, at first you do not like my father, now he is hokay. At first you do not like me—now you like me, a little?'"

"And what did he say? What did he say?"

"He said he does not like me."

It took only the crack of the wood on the ball, sounding

like a thunderbolt in the stillness of the afternoon, to tell the hushed crowd that it would never see the ball again. In an instant it plummeted behind the four hundred and fifteen-foot fence backing the center-field bleachers. As Durham rounded the turn at third base, close behind the tying run, he executed a mock ballet vault made grotesque by his huge size. When he leaped on the plate and into the arms of his teammates, thousands were pushing into the exits but most of the others sat down again, stunned and unable to accept what had happened.

Tasia grabbed Miss Wiley's arm. "We have lose! We have lose!" she shouted plaintively.

Miss Wiley seemed not to hear. "He said he didn't like you? He told you that?"

Ambassador Galynin strode out of the box, expressionless and staring straight ahead. Sobolev followed, and behind them came Bukharov and Malsynenko. No one said a word, but Malsynenko directed a quick look at Tasia as he passed her side, and there was a sternness in his eyes.

Tasia resumed her seat and then looked at Miss Wiley, who was still standing, and despite the sadness of what had just happened a blush of mischief glowed on her face as she spoke: "He said: 'I do not like you, Tasia. I love you.'"

Later, waiting for Deborin in the club lounge, Tasia walked slowly to the window and looked at the honeycomb of empty seats beyond the outfield. "It is so sad that we are winning," she said, "and then we lose. I think now of Bunny. I feel much sadness for him."

Miss Wiley joined her at the window. "I'm thinking of your father," she said.

12

Other hotels in Los Angeles had fancier pictures on the walls and better air-conditioning, but Horace Bratton liked this one because the rooms had at least one chair that was made, perhaps measured, for guests with manly rumps. He squirmed a little deeper into it and leaned back on its comfort, listening to the ricochet of night noises from Hollywood Boulevard. And when the quaint, disconnected musing flounced into his thoughts he almost laughed out loud.

It had been quite some time since he had thanked God for anything and here he was—in his shorts and with his tired feet making cool rubs on the carpet—saying thank God for the Communists.

Great hounds of heaven, he thought, what would his sainted mother—rest her soul—say to that? A sacrilege, that's what she would say.

Sacrilege or not, the Communists had given him much to be thankful for.

Not that he might not be where he was without them, but a man had to face reality. Those Reds certainly had changed things around in his life.

Bratton would hardly discuss this with anyone but himself, but until the Soviet government took over the team he had just about resigned himself to the probability that he would occupy but an ordinary niche in the annals of the game. The reputation he had acquired over the years was that of a hard-working manager, but a nice-fellow type whose conduct on and off the field lacked the shades of color that separate the man from the character. And while he had spent a respectable part of his career in the first division, being close to a pennant now and then was something only he and not the multitudes would remember, for in baseball there is no second prize. He often reflected that having never won a pennant, and not being flamboyant, the recognition that posterity likely would give him would be simply that of a one-armed manager.

But the picture certainly had changed since that rainy afternoon in Yankee Stadium when the Deputy Chairman of the Central Council of the All-Union Committee on Sports and Culture had shown up in the dugout for work, the pockets of his raincoat bulging with bubble-gum cards.

Here he was, not only a pennant winner for the first time in his life but actually in the lair of the enemy with a delicious three-to-one game lead in the World Series. And this was only part of the attainment.

In New York, Cliff Brayner, dean of the baseball writers, had conjectured that the Baseball Writers' Association of America would probably select him "Manager of the Year" (even though, technically, he was the assistant manager to Deborin). Then in the last week of September, in one of those coincidences that seldom happen even to the heads of state, he had made the cover of both *Newsweek* and *Time*. Next, in feelers that were about as subtle as a three-base blast, he had been offered the manager's post by two other teams in the American League (with an invitation to name his own salary in each instance), and finally a major publishing house was after him to do a book, at season's end, on his astonishing odyssey with Mikhail Deborin. Suddenly he was flamboyant.

But even more precious to him was what the incredible turn of events had done to his personal life. The challenge and agitation brought on by the Russian ownership of the team had rekindled in his wife, Dorothy, an interest in his

work that had long been on the wane. She had emerged
from a strange depression that had started to close in two
years ago and resumed her old habit, one she enjoyed, of
coming to the park to watch him in action, and as a result
the lonely days of seclusion at home and at the movies had
come to an end for her, and the warmth that had been
between them before was back again.

Indeed, the Communists had given him cause to be grateful, he mused contentedly. Even old Bukharov was doing
his share—so long as he stayed out of sight. For it was a
remarkable fact, especially during the September race to the
wire, that the White Sox wins went up in relation to the
times that Bukharov went out of town. And now the pattern
was setting into a dramatic climax during the World Series,
for with Bukharov sitting in the front tier during the first
game in Chicago, the Sox had bowed to the Dodgers. But
Bukharov had taken off on another of his mysterious trips
that very night, whereupon the Sox had come roaring back
the next day with an eleven-to-one bombardment. Two
days later on their home grounds, the Dodgers inexplicably
came down with a massive case of galloping errors—com-
mitting seven on a familiar infield—and gave it away, six
to three. The fourth game, with Bukharov still mercifully
absent, developed into a four-four marathon that ended
with a fifty-six-thousand-voice groan joggling the walls
of Dodger Stadium when the Chicagoans loaded the bases
in the last of the twelfth then watched, mouths agape, as
Dodger pitcher Ross Harvey walked across the winning
run on four consecutive balls.

For Bratton, this was a time to enjoy the ecstasy that had
escaped him so long, for now there was only one more to
win, and it could be tomorrow. But even if it were not
tomorrow, the Dodgers would still be against the wall for
then the duel would shift back to Chicago with the Sox
still a game ahead in their own backyard. He closed his
eyes and wiggled his toes and, as he often did the night
before a game, he began to play tomorrow's game in his

mind. Alternately, he frowned and bit his lip and smiled through the first two innings, and he was going into the third with a one-run lead when the sharp rap on the door forced him to call time. That would be Deborin, of course, for it was time for his nightly call. He would walk in, looking exhausted as usual, complain that he couldn't get to sleep and inquire, as usual, if "all our chickens are into the chicken house for the night." Then they would make small talk, or big talk, and sometimes small talk that became big talk (such as the night of Bratton's mortification when Deborin schooled him on the German origin of the hot dog which Bratton had been extolling as another of the great American inventions). Then Deborin would bid him *dobraia noch'* and return to his room. The visits had become a ritual when the team was on the road, and Bratton had come to look forward to them each night.

Deborin shuffled in, running a hand through his shaggy mane, but he made no mention of his insomnia nor the late show he would normally have been watching.

He sat on the edge of Bratton's bed. "I have been talking at the distant telephone," he said. "Comrade Bukharov, he called."

Bratton gave his bare knee a slap of disgust. "I knew it was too good to last," he said.

"Too good?"

"I just wish he'd keep away from us. Everything's been going so good and I was hoping he'd be out of the country, or something."

"He was out of the country, but he is returned. He was in Havana."

The chill of the California night was moving in through the open window, and Bratton walked to the clothes closet and put on his robe. "It's too bad he didn't stay there for another week," he said.

Deborin lifted one leg and clasped his hands around his knee. "He wants me to at once come to Chicago."

"He must be crazy!"

"I tell to him of the important tomorrow, but he directs I take a very soon airplane and come to Chicago."

"Good God! What's the matter with him!"

Deborin looked down at the floor for a moment, and a silvery tousle slipped over his eyes. "It is all much strange," he said. "I demand why I must come when we have the important tomorrow, but he tells to me only I must be at the airport, the O'Hare, at seven o'clock in the night."

"Real mysterious, isn't he?"

Deborin smiled for the first time. "He tells to me I will see something that will shake the teeth of the Americans," he said.

Bratton went to the window, peered into the darkness below for a moment, and closed it. "Big deal," he said.

"He has made to assemble all the representatives of the press, and he will tell important things for all the world," Deborin went on.

Bratton bit his lip again. "But why the airport?" he asked.

"I do not know. He tells to me only I must be there to make greetings for some peoples, much important peoples, which will come there in the night."

Slowly a realization took shape in Bratton's mind. "I think I get it," he said. "Some of your big shots are coming in from Russia for the rest of the Series."

"Maybe it is this," Deborin said. "But if we are triumphant tomorrow they will not be here where the climax is."

"No. But they probably figure we've got it wrapped up and they're coming for the big do in Chicago, you know—all those crazy medals you people are always handing out."

Deborin smiled. "Perhaps you are correct. This is much confidence from my people, is it not?"

"You said it. So you're leaving?"

Deborin put his fingers over his eyes and massaged them. He was tired. "I am not leaving," he said.

Bratton sat up. "You're not!"

"No. My place, it is here. I stay here."

"Great!" Bratton exclaimed. "I bet that shook up Bukharov."

"He tells to me my presence is commanded by the Ambassador. But I tell to him my judgment is I stay here until my work here it is finished."

Bratton was delighted. "You've got guts, Mike," he said. "I like that. But I sure wonder what this is all about."

Deborin rose to leave. "We shall have a report when we return to Chicago that is—how do you say?—from the mouth of the horses. I have talked at the distant telephone to Tasia. Her sickness is finished now and she is out of the bed, so I tell her to go to the airport and to be our eyes, our ears."

"Good," Bratton said. "That's good." He padded into the clothes closet again, looking for his slippers. "Nothing rattles you, does it?"

"Rattles?"

"Nothing bothers you."

The Commissar opened the door, then turned around. "But yes," he said.

"Like what?"

"The Dodgers of Los Angeles."

The taxi made a broad, circling sweep on a light-spangled arc of the tollway as O'Hare Airport came into view, and the driver felt sad that the trip was already ending. It had been a long time since he'd had such a fascinating fare—those two oddball dames yammering away in the back seat about Russia and baseball and love and getting deported and commissars and ambassadors and guys like that. And the one with the sniffles, the pretty one, she had to be Russian the way she was going on about this guy and that guy in Moscow. He wondered, with a secret thrill making throbs on his stomach, if the conversation might have something to do with espionage and he wondered if he should talk to somebody about it. But they had mentioned Bunny a lot, and Beadle was an idol of his (even if he hadn't gotten a hit this afternoon) and it was fantastic to think that his hero could be mixed up with an international spy ring, and so he dismissed the thought from his mind and concentrated on the rear-view mirror which carried an exotic close-up of the foreign job as she huddled in her white polo coat. She sure was a knockout, he thought, even with a runny nose.

The runny nose, brought on by a ferocious cold, had kept Tasia from making the trip to Los Angeles (a disappointment that prompted Miss Wiley, who dreaded flying, to remain with her in Chicago), but missing the West Coast games was not what depressed her during the drive from the Loop. Nor was it the five-to-one defeat the Sox had suffered that afternoon in Los Angeles. It was the vengeful threat to emasculate the team which Bukharov had voiced to Beadle, and it was her fear of what lurked ahead that she confided to Miss Wiley as they rode in the early autumn darkness. While the First Secretary had not spelled out precisely what he would do, he had vowed that Beadle and his "bourgeois friends"—whatever that meant—would not be on the team next season. He had been vague on how he would bring this about, but he had made it clear to Beadle that he had received approval, presumably from Moscow, to dismiss any player for whatever reason he chose and to take the steps he deemed necessary to bring up replacements. She was quite sure that only she and Bunny knew of the menacing crisis, for she had not dared upset her father with it when he was embarking on the World Series, and she was thankful that the rest of the team was unaware of the turmoil. But she was tormented by self-reproach because she felt that the upheaval would not have come about had she not become involved with Bunny.

"Perhaps Bukharov is correct," she said. "Perhaps all would be well if I was at my home, and not in this country."

"Nonsense!" Miss Wiley said. "Don't talk like that. You're not responsible for what happened."

"But I know that Bukharov and the others are angry because I have a friendship with Bunny, and with you, and with Mr. Bratton, and not with them."

"What of it? Let them think what they want. This is a free country, isn't it?"

Tasia looked out the window of the cab at the airport lights flickering in the distance, and a wistful look came into her eyes. "Yes," she said, "but it is not my country."

Miss Wiley sensed the suggestion of affront in what she had said, and she took Tasia's hand in hers. "I'm sorry," she said. "I didn't mean that the way it sounded. But doesn't it show that we look on you as one of us?"

She released Tasia's hand and cringed in the seat a little as the piercing whine of a departing jet seemed to drum on the roof of the cab. "The main thing," she said, as the roar tapered off, "is to stop taking the blame for anything that's happened. Bukharov and his gang want you to feel this way, but everybody knows he was making trouble for the team and your father long before you and Bunny knew each other."

"That is true," Tasia said, "but perhaps what he is doing now would not be if we did not become in love."

"Dear me, Tasia, I think you're worrying for nothing. We don't know for sure that anything really bad is going to happen, do we?"

"I do not have the good feeling you have. Bukharov is very mysterious; he has been making many trips away from this country and I have a fear that this—what he has arranged for tonight, it will be bad for all."

The cab moved cautiously as it began to circle the vast parking lot on the way to the terminal. Miss Wiley refused to be downcast.

"I think everything's going to be just fine," she said. "You have a man who loves you and—who knows?—he might ask you to marry him, and if you marry him nobody can send you away. Not ten like Bukharov could send you away."

For the first time since they had entered the taxi, Tasia smiled. "Yes," she said, "it would be very nice."

As she often did in moments like these, since they brought her as close to romance as she would ever come and since she was so fond of Tasia, Miss Wiley felt happy for her and elated, and even a little giddy. "You'll think I'm an old nosy," she tittered, "but if Bunny asks you, do you think— well, would you marry him?"

Tasia felt silent for a long moment and a look of serenity and bliss came into her large, lavender eyes and Miss Wiley thought she had never appeared so beautiful.

"I would say yes to him," she said finally, "because I love him in a truly way. But I wish that I can be certain that he, also, loves me in a truly way."

Miss Wiley felt her fingers rubbing together again, although not as enjoyably this time because of the gloves she was wearing. "Oh, dear!" she said, a laughing lilt in her voice. "You're wondering if it's true love for Bunny? You must be the last one to know!"

The cab slid into a vacant slot in front of the main doors to the terminal, and Tasia uncrossed her legs, frowning. "I do not understand," she said.

Miss Wiley made no effort this time to conceal her skittishness. "Well," she laughed, "everybody else around knows it, so it's high time you knew it too, young lady."

"They know?"

"Of course they know!" Miss Wiley said. "As the story goes—and everybody was talking about it—you evidently said something to Bunny about that revolting tobacco he was chewing. Well, from that moment on, he quit. And he'd had the habit for nine years!"

She patted Tasia's arm. "And that, my dear, has to be true love."

In the memory of most of the veteran newsmen on hand for Stepan Bukharov's press conference, there had never been anything like it. It was hard to believe that one man, a foreigner without the savvy for such things, was able to bring off as smooth a production as the one set up on the ramp at Gate Five. It was, as one of them remarked, like something out of Hollywood and even there it would have challenged the skills of a platoon of experienced promoters and press agents. How Bukharov, apparently working alone and handicapped by frequent trips out of the country, had managed to bring this much care and detail to his affair was an achievement for which, intolerable as he was, he had to be admired. He had even had the thoughtfulness to counter the chill of the October night with two huge urns of coffee, next to which reposed a massive bouquet of chrys-anthemums (the purpose of which made for lively specula-tion).

It was a credit to Bukharov's ingenuity that almost fifty newsmen and photographers, along with a strong comple-ment from the television and radio networks, had answered his summons to O'Hare Airport, and it was considered significant by some that lofty, influential Edwin Tripp, most powerful of the syndicated columnists, had condescended to leave his Washington aerie and grace the event with his personal presence. It was claimed (though never con-firmed) that the last time Tripp, who employed a small army of legmen, had deigned to attend a press conference was on Armistice Day.

Not the least of Bukharov's accomplishments was securing permission from the airport authorities to conduct a mass press conference on the ramp near the area reserved for the loading of planes. At this spot, in a roped-off section, he had set up a small platform on which stood a cluster of micro-phones. Directly in front was an exclusive row of chairs on which sat Ambassador Leonid Galynin and the Russian trade attaché from the embassy, Valentin Kononov—on his knees the briefcase he carried everywhere but never seemed to open. Next to them sat Russell Kirk, the Commissioner of Baseball, his pink face aglow in the swath of television lights set up near the speakers' stand; Arnold Lang, president of the American League; Vernon Crowley, president of the National League (both of whom had been piqued enough by Bukharov's telegram to fly in from Los Angeles); Herman Bradley, interim president of the corporation established to reorganize Childers' holdings; tall, solemn Leonard Daniels, Childers' former chief counsel; Tom Morris, his fidgety, pipe-smoking aide, and Lionel Harris, counsel for the Baseball Commission. Behind them, in neat rows of ten, were the chairs for the newsmen—giving the scene the appearance of a small open-air theater. A full, near-scarlet harvest moon hovered overhead, and a few in the group were willing to bet that Bukharov had ordered that too.

At precisely seven o'clock—Miss Wiley set her watch by the light of the moon when she saw Bukharov frowning at his—Bukharov mounted the one step to the platform and introduced his ambassador. Smiling and removing his pince-nez, Galynin thanked the audience for coming to the press conference, explained that his part in the proceedings would consist only of greeting a group of "distinguished arrivals," and turned the program over to Bukharov.

Bukharov, making a vain attempt to shield his eyes from the strong lights, plucked a sheet of white paper from his inside coat pocket. In front of him, Kirk's hoarse cough smashed the silence irreverently.

"Ladies and gentlemen," Bukharov said into the microphones. "First I say this, and I ask your indulgence. It will not be permitted to you to ask questions from Ambassador Galynin and from me. In a little time it will be permitted to you to ask questions from another person. I hope your cooperation. But so you will know why you have been asked to come to this place, I read to you now a prepared statement for the taking of the notes."

He brought the paper close to his thick glasses, and read slowly:

"On this night, at the hour approximately of eight o'clock, a airplane of the Republic of Cuba will arrive at O'Hare Airport of Chicago. On this airplane there contains twenty-four professional players of baseball which will become the members of the Chicago Belye Chulki. These athletes—"

A gasp swept suddenly through the small crowd, and Bukharov waited for it to subside. In a sudden, distracted gesture Tasia seized Miss Wiley's arm and cried, "Oh, no!" Miss Wiley closed her eyes, and shuddered.

"These athletes," he resumed, "come here in a voluntary decision at the request of their government, prepared to do their duty for the glory of their fatherland. They will not take part in the continuation of the activities that are current, but they will live here to become familiar with the organization and operations of the sport in this country, in preparation of the activities of next year.

"Next year, the American athletes who are now members of the Chicago Belye Chulki will no longer be members of the club. There will not be renewal of their contracts. This development marks another evidence of the cooperation and goodwill between the Republic of Cuba and the Union of the Soviet Socialist Republics."

Bukharov paused, looking up from his paper at the newsmen, and there was the semblance of a smile on his thin lips. "For the taking of the notes, I have some statistics which I understand are important to American journalists."

He consulted his statement again: "In the party of arrivals from Cuba there contains twenty-four players of baseball, and ten wifes of the players. There is also twenty-three children of the players, nineteen mothers of the players, fourteen fathers, thirty-three brothers and sisters, and nine grandfathers and grandmothers by a total of one hundred and thirty-two. Also in the group"—here Bukharov permitted himself a wry smile—"one includes three dogs and one cat.

"The party is under the leadership of Comrade Carlos Machado who, as is well known, is hailed now and before as the most successful player of baseball in the Republic of Cuba. Comrade Machado has agreed to serve as the spokesman for his compatriots, and it will be permitted to the

journalists to ask questions from him. This is the end of the
official statement . . . and now we await the arrival of the
airplane."

When the newsmen returned from calling in their first
bulletins to their offices, they converged on Bukharov despite his insistence that he would have no comment beyond
that contained in his prepared statement. He took to fend-
ing off each shouted, angry query by pointing to the sky
and saying grimly: "There are your answers." The exasper-
ated reporters, unable to record Commissioner Kirk's reac-
tions because they could not find him (Kirk had prudently
found refuge in one of the airport restaurants, there to
partake of precautions against the risks of a cold), tried
pumping Lang and Crowley but the league officials were
simply too baffled to venture opinions, and eventually the
newsmen fell to interviewing each other until finally Bukharov was able to point his arm on the ground instead of in
the air and shout above the roaring throb of the jet as it
lumbered slowly toward them: "Here are your answers!"

It seemed to take an interminably long time for the door
to open but finally, as if someone had punched a hole
through a towering silver foil, it swung outward and behind
the stewardess stepped a stubby man with broad shoulders
and a bronzed face who started to wave at the three Russians waiting for him at the bottom of the ramp then, self-
consciously, put his hand in his pocket. As he reached the
bottom, he shook hands with Bukharov, then with Galynin
and Kononov, and introduced his wife, a handsome woman
even shorter than he was, and the sports-minded among the
Americans in the roped-off area recognized him as Carlos
Machado, known in the Cuban leagues as "the destroyer"
for being the only man to pitch five no-hitters—two of them
in one season.

Machado walked between Galynin and Kononov toward
the platform as Bukharov escorted the Cuban's wife to a
chair in the front row, next to Morris who became so nervous again he absent-mindedly slipped his finger inside his

pipe, giving it a painful burn. Both the Machados now were unsmiling. Bukharov then took his position in front of the microphones and waited until the rest of the travelers, several of them with mewing, crying infants in their arms, had filed into a semicircular group behind the stand. The children were laughing and shouting, but their elders seemed exceptionally solemn. Finally all was silence and the glow of the low-hanging moon was so bright that the television lights seemed to intrude. Bukharov cleared his throat.

"Ladies and gentlemen," he said, "I thank you for your patience. As you perhaps have conclude, this is Comrade Carlos Machado, the brilliant athlete of the Republic of Cuba. Here also is the charming Madame Machado that you will meet later. But before, Comrade Machado will talk a statement and will answer the questions of the journalists."

As Machado advanced to the microphones, Bukharov left the platform with what seemed to be an unusually gay step, gathered up the flowers near the urns and, nodding knowingly at Machado's wife as if to confide the tribute in store for her, returned to stand by the muscular Cuban. Tasia and Miss Wiley exchanged glances, but no message passed between them. For a full half minute Machado stood there, uttering not a word, as if groping for thought, and in a moment of silence strange for an airport the only sound was the scratching of pencils on paper. He gave his wife an odd look, as if he were staring at a stranger, then turned and shot a quick glance at his people behind him. Finally, his fists clenching and loosening, he began to speak in unexpectedly good English:

"What I must say is difficult . . . because I speak not only for myself but for many. But I must say it. . . ."

He glanced at Bukharov whose face was almost completely hidden by the flowers he was carrying, and then looked at the floor. "What I must say is not something that has now just happened. I—we talked of this in the voyage, but it is something all of us had in our—in our hearts a long time. We also talked of it together before the voyage, among the families. And we have prayed . . . We have prayed very much . . . because we love our homeland very much . . . But we know that not any more can we live under the dictatorship that now makes the people slaves . . . We wish very much to have freedom, and so—"

There was a harsh grating of chairs on the pavement as several men suddenly stood up in the aisles, and toward the back a photographer threw his paper cup to the ground and raced to the platform. Miss Wiley brought her hand to her mouth, suppressing an outcry.

"—and so," Machado continued, his voice loud and no longer hesitant, "we . . . all of us who are here tonight . . . ask asylum in the United States of America!"

Machado's last words were drowned out in the pandemonium that followed. A dozen or more newsmen bolted their seats and hurdled the rope on their way to telephones—one older man choosing to duck underneath, thereby raising it flush into the stomach of an airborne unfortunate who somersaulted into the asphalt with a sickening thud. Three or four of the running reporters suddenly decided they had questions to ask, and they spun about and raced back, causing collisions and inspiring oaths that forced Miss Wiley to turn her head away. Amid the shouts and the jostling, Machado leaped toward his wife, grabbed her by the arm and led her, half-running, to the back of the platform where his people stood. Without saying a word, both fell to their knees and placed their lips to the ground and, as if by signal, every adult in the Cuban group fell to the ground and kissed it. In the mounting commotion Bukharov had stood motionless, as if frozen and not believing what he had heard and seen. Abruptly he came to life again; his eyes darted about wildly, looking for a place to deposit the chrysanthemums, and finding himself hemmed in by the shouting, shoving, cursing mob he flung the flowers into the air and they made an eerie sight as they separated amid the popping flash bulbs and drifted down upon the surging crowd. One of the blooms came to rest on Morris' hat and he was so taken aback that his teeth unclenched and his pipe dropped into the maze of swirling feet. Bukharov finally spotted an opening in the shuffle and squirmed through it to get to Machado and as he did he nudged one of the microphones which toppled onto Galynin's forehead, stunning him momentarily and sending the pince-nez sliding off his nose. With the reporters in close pursuit, Bukharov scudded up to Machado and the one hundred and thirty-one other Cubans and he stood before them, panting and trying to catch his breath, and between the moonlight and the reflections in the windows of the observation deck above, his complexion seemed to take on a purplish tinge.

"Traitors!" he shouted. "Swine! Have you no shame?"

Machado was calm now. He stood immobile, his arms crossed on his chest and his wife at his side, and behind him his people stood as firm as their leader, silent and unsmiling.

"It is better," Machado said gently to Bukharov, "that I do not discuss with you at this time." He turned to the newsmen who were pressing on him both to record his words and to get away from the television dollies that were rolling perilously close, cameras trained on the refugees. "I hope you will understand," he told them, "that I cannot say no more. We are asking your government to help us, and so it is better that we first speak only to the representatives of your government."

Aging Edwin Tripp, who had managed to remain dignified and unruffled throughout the tumult, stepped forward from the side. "Mr. Machado," he rumbled, "it is very important that you be put in touch with the proper authorities immediately. If you will come with me to a telephone, we'll get started at once."

Bukharov's rage was beyond control. "Cretins!" he screamed at the Cubans, shaking his fist in the air. "Manure of diseased goats!! You are here as hypocrites! You deceive your superiors with the agreements to come here! You have betrayed your Republic!"

Machado turned his back on Bukharov and began to speak to his people in comforting terms, in their language, and the newsmen hovered around Bukharov—some to try to calm him down, others to question him. Bukharov continued to shriek at the defectors. "The Soviet government will not stand for this! You will be taken back to Cuba and punished —all of you beasts! We shall start proceedings tonight!"

A half-dozen airport policemen filed out of a door below the observation deck and moved briskly toward the disturbance. Back in the roped-off section, Ambassador Galynin was on his hands and knees, groping amid the toppled chairs, and suddenly he found himself eyeball to eyeball with Morris who was also on his hands and knees.

"Have you seen a pipe?" Morris asked, his hat askew.

"No," the Ambassador said. "Have you seen a pince-nez?"

"No," said Morris, and they crawled past each other.

Commissioner Kirk, who was standing nearby with Lang and Crowley, surveyed the bizarre tableau and said: "I think we all need a drink."

A sharp, near-wintry wind began to blow in from across the runways as Tasia and Miss Wiley, hugging their coats about them, walked away from the ramp. As they reached the passenger door leading into the terminal, Miss Wiley turned and looked at the sky once more. "It's really a beautiful moon, isn't it?" she said.

Tasia looked at her watch. "Bunny is flying home now," she said, an intimate smile playing on her face. "I hope he is looking at it too."

13

The day after the arrival of the Cuban defectors (Tripp had gleefully dubbed them the "switch hitters") was the day that baseball went from national pastime to international crisis. True to Bukharov's threat, the Russian and Cuban embassies lost no time reporting the catastrophe to their respective governments. By the time the ball players and their frightened, confused wives, children, mothers, fathers, brothers, sisters, and grandparents had been whisked from the airport to a suburban motel, Havana was talking excitedly to Moscow. By the time the bedraggled exiles had sorted out their nightclothes, Havana was listening meekly to Moscow. And by mid-morning the Cuban Ambassador in Washington had personally delivered a strongly worded protest to the State Department. It charged in the most indignant terms that the runaway citizens of the Republic had been brainwashed, in some way not specified, by "despicable anarchists" in the homeland who were paid agents of the Central Intelligence Agency.

From that moment on, events moved with such stunning swiftness that for a full twenty-four hours it appeared as if the world were holding its breath, tensed for the after-shocks of a thunderclap that had caused tremors in the principal capitals. It was almost a time of standing still (including the Dodgers who arrived in a somber, silent Chicago—the populace inside, glued to newscasts—and wondered if they were in the right town).

Little more than an hour after receiving the Cuban Embassy's protest, the State Department issued a brief, terse statement rejecting its contents as gross distortion of facts. The speed of Washington's reply stamped it as an unmistakable rebuff. When it was followed immediately by a White House announcement that the President would make no comment on the incident, Galynin, now commanding behind the scene, pulled the pin on the first diplomatic grenade and gave it to Cuba to lob. Shortly after noon Ramon Mendiata, leader of the Cuban delegation to the United Nations, was making a formal demand on the Security Council that it begin immediate deliberations on the dispute since it constituted a breach of international ethics and a danger to the security of his country, and posed a clear threat to peace on the North American continent. Prepared and delivered in surprising haste, Mendiata's indictment denounced the United States for unlawfully harboring "renegades and criminals" wanted by their government, and called on the Security Council's aid to effect their surrender.

The United States was held to a frustrating silence since it occupied one of the five permanent seats in the Council, and the UN charter prohibited a permanent member from voting in a dispute to which it was a party. The Soviet Union agreed with a joint opinion from the United Kingdom and France that international peace and security were not in imminent danger—a move which won it sympathetic desk-thumping from the Council's six non-permanent members. Fortified by this acclaim for its show of goodwill, the Soviet Union then cannily moved that the matter be referred to the General Assembly for debate. Opposed by the United Kingdom, France, and China (with the United States forced to abstain), the motion was supported by the six non-permanent members and carried with the seven affirmative votes it needed. The rotating members felt that a compromise was in order and saw the issue as one on which the General Assembly would not be likely to deliberate for months, giving the United States and Cuba time to settle their dispute privately.

But that was not the way Mendiata and the Moscow masterminds tugging at his strings saw it. For in a rare coincidence, Cuba was already before the General Assembly with a similar complaint involving five other fugitives from the Republic who, months before, had found refuge in the Florida Keys. The five were army officers who had stolen away in a fishing smack and for the past two days the General Assembly had been listening to Mendiata's demand that they be extradited as deserters. Now, since he still had the floor, it would be a simple matter for Mendiata to incorporate the new incident into the standing complaint as further evidence of American perfidy.

And that was precisely what Mendiata did the next day, a day that brought to Chicago a raw foretaste of winter with rain-drenched Canadian winds howling across Lake Michigan with such fury that the sixth World Series game had to be postponed.

Outwardly, Mendiata gave the impression of a formidable enemy. He was barrel-chested and almost six feet tall, with a scarred cheek and shiny black hair combed straight back. To some, he conveyed the picture of a nightclub bouncer who would never call for reinforcements, and at his desk in the General Assembly he sat as tall as others stood. But it was a deceptive appearance for he was a mild, almost shy man with an embarrassing handicap that he strove mightily to conceal: he suffered from stage fright and when the spectator galleries were packed, as they were now, he felt uncomfortable and sometimes cut his speeches short to avoid the clammy feel of public gaze.

To ease his task, now, as he spoke, he refrained from looking at the dreaded galleries and concentrated on the President of the General Assembly, Sir Percy Candliffe of New Zealand. Sir Percy, a man of gentle bearing with flowing white hair that gave him the pastoral look of a contented poet, understood Mendiata's problem and gave him reassuring nods to relieve his anguish.

With this encouragement, Mendiata made a facile transition from the pending issue of the five army deserters to that of the mass defection of the baseball contingent. He reiterated the charges of CIA brainwashing, but before launching into new demands for the refugees' surrender, he chose to dwell on the enormity of their offense by explaining the importance of baseball and the stature of professional players in his country. At this point, the delegate from Thailand rose to a point of personal curiosity: was baseball, he wondered, the national sport of Cuba?

Well, Mendiata replied, almost—but not quite. If one were to be technical one would have to concede that, historically, jai-alai was Cuba's national sport. But the rise of interest in baseball, he continued, had been such that one could properly describe it as a national phenomenon—and the delegate from Thailand would appreciate the influence of a beloved recreation on the morale of the citizenry.

The delegate from Thailand rose again to declare that he certainly appreciated that fact. Indeed, his own country's principal recreation had for centuries been an important factor in the national way of life. That popular pastime, for the benefit of Assembly members unaware of it, was kite-fighting—wherein one player flew a "male" kite while his opponent flew a "female" kite. The object of the game, he went on, was for the "male" kite to knock the "female" out of the air while the "female" defended herself, so to speak, and counterattacked to drive the "male" aggressor out of the air.

The report on what Thailanders did in their spare time prompted the delegate from Sweden to beg the floor to voice his country's pride in the invigorating sport of curling. He had barely begun to describe the game when the delegate from the Netherlands was on his feet. If the delegate from Sweden was suggesting that curling had originated in his country, he said, he was—with all respect for an esteemed neighbor—in error. The Netherlands, he asserted, was responsible for giving curling to the world (despite the specious claims of Scottish historians), and further, the Netherlands had also originated ice skating. Indeed, to this day schools in the Netherlands declared a holiday when the canals froze over.

Mendiata had been pleased with the original interruption, for it had afforded him a little time to assemble his thoughts. But now he wondered how he would regain the floor; small beads of perspiration appeared on his neck.

As the Netherlander resumed his seat Mendiata coughed discreetly into his microphone, but nothing emerged and his mouth stayed open when he discovered that the delegate from Canada was already standing. Mention of ice skating, the Canadian said, reminded him of the vast import of hockey on his country's recreational life. But lest the Assembly assume that hockey was Canada's national game, he hastened to explain that the honor went to lacrosse thanks to an act of Parliament. And lacrosse, it should be made clear, was the stepchild of baggataway—rugged relaxation of Canada's first Indians.

Mendiata squirmed in his seat, and the beads on the back of his neck were beginning to roll onto his collar. He placed his hands on the top of his desk and began to rise, but the delegate from Ireland beat him to it with a dissertation on hurling as played there centuries before the arrival of Saint Patrick.

Now the scramble was on as the fever of national pride swept through the Assembly, and delegate after delegate rose to weave a paean of praise for his country's sports and recreations. Mendiata, now absolutely bewildered, was unable to halt the unshackled eloquence for fear of alienating the support of the diplomats—even though they were all but trampling his theme into oblivion. In a round-robin of patriotic vainglory, the bored galleries were assailed with long homilies on bicycling in France, bullfighting in Spain, cricket in England, sumo in Japan, karagiosis in Greece,

Arabian horse racing in Saudi Arabia, chess in Iran, wayang in Indonesia, cockfights in several South American republics (with variations on the rules), and folk dancing in Nepal (for the natives—climbing Mount Everest for the tourists). At one point, as the monologs droned on, Mendiata gave Sir Percy a woeful look of supplication, as if imploring him to shut off the long-winded palaver. But, to his horror, the President of the General Assembly was fast asleep.

At length, the autumnal dusk thumped on the glassy escarpments of Manhattan as the delegate from one of the emerging nations finished describing his people's most popular recreation—attending tribal weddings and toasting the bride and groom for three days and nights. This speech over, hunger roused Sir Percy from his slumber and he adjourned the debate until the morrow.

As Mendiata strode out of the chamber, his delegation at his heels, it was his misfortune to overhear a bearded Ethiopian trying to explain American baseball's double-play to a turbaned Hindu. A wince rippled the tired lines on his face. It had been a very long day.

The next day—again one of wretched weather that once more suspended the World Series—was also a long one for Mendiata, but more favorable to his cause. Despite its derailment the previous day, he deftly put it back on the track and received the solid support of the delegates from Poland and Yugoslavia whose speeches took up the morning debate. Rebuttal got under way at the afternoon session with Gerald Fulton, head of the American delegation, making his country's first formal reply to the Cuban charge. He was followed by the delegate from Italy, Primo Ferrini, who not only absolved the United States of blame in the Cuban incident but angrily accused the Soviet Union of using it for its own ends to perpetuate the cold war—a selfish strategy, he thundered, which revolted the non-Communist world. At this, the Soviet Union's crusty Leon Sobolev jumped to his feet and called Ferrini a fawning parrot for the decadent West. Ferrini retorted by accusing Sobolev of scheming to sabotage baseball because his country didn't know how to play it. And before Sir Percy had a chance to moderate the rancor, the Italian and the Russian were shouting at each other from across the chamber.

This was the first explosion of the debate and, as he sometimes did in tense moments, Archibald Blondahl, the genial delegate from Australia, uncoiled his long legs from behind his desk and rose to a point of order. Blondahl simply detested loud arguments and he had a mischievous talent for cooling tempers by changing the subject while still dangling it before his listeners. It was his earnest hope, he said, that cool heads would prevail and nothing would occur to work a hardship on sports which was, after all, at the root of the dispute. It would be a pity if a sport with the appeal that baseball enjoyed should be hurt by foreigners—especially Italians and Russians who might not appreciate its finer points. He knew whereof he spoke, for while nothing could touch the thrill of a good cricket match, he had, during his six years of diplomatic service in America, become something of a baseball fan.

Even during the game's frequent dull moments, Blondahl went on, a sly twinkle appearing in his eyes, he enjoyed going to baseball parks because there he encountered such peculiar types of fans—odd characters to delight the student of human nature. Indeed, he had them categorized by traits and could usually count on observing a typical specimen at almost any game. Just a fortnight ago, for example, three very fine specimens sat in the row he occupied. One was the stage-struck type who missed most of the action because he spent the time preening himself in case the cameras should pan his way and he would get a chance to wave. The other two were opposites—one dreaded the camera because the lady he had brought to the park was not his wife, the other feared it because he was forever telling his boss he was attending a relative's funeral (indeed, he had buried his grandmother six times this season and was currently working on his grandfather).

Blondahl lumbered on, ticking off a long list of other favorite types—the gregarious clod who started off by borrowing one's program and wound up borrowing money for a lemonade; the hero-worshiper whose second cousin by marriage knew the uncle of one of the players, and the compulsive eater who attended games solely because it was the only place where he could stuff himself peacefully, away from his wife's nagging.

Blondahl nodded in the direction of Fulton's group. "I trust the Americans will not mind my twitting their baseball fans," he said, smiling, "for actually the most peculiar fan of them all is my wife. For years she has accompanied me to the parks and I have spent countless hours explaining the game to her. But alas, my efforts have failed; to this day she still thinks that Early Wynn means taking the first game of a double-header."

The Americans broke into laughter and most of the other delegates followed suit, including those who, like the Australian's wife, had not the slightest idea what Early Wynn, and the rest of the speech, was all about. Sobolev and his men stared stonily ahead.

"Be that as it may," Blondahl wound up, "I hope this dreadful weather lets up and the World Series resumes to-morrow. I am ruddy well interested. Aren't we all?"

Blondahl's wish, echoing that of millions of impatient Americans, was realized. The rains subsided that night and while the prospect was for damp and slippery grounds, the game was on.

Not on, however, was the morning session of the General Assembly because of the funeral of a New York ex-Senator and one-time chairman of the UN's Trusteeship Council. But when the Assembly convened for the afternoon debate, Leon Sobolev was the first man at his desk—with a thirty-eight page speech and a number of empty seats in front of him. He thought it strange that there should be so many absentees, since the chamber was generally crowded when the chief of the Soviet Union delegation was scheduled for a major address. But he shrugged it off with the assumption that the forenoon recess had prompted some delegates to skip the entire day.

Speaking in Russian, Sobolev made short shrift of the Cuban defectors as baseball players and quickly established his message as one of profound shock that the United States would even consider granting asylum to dishonored, discredited turncoats, at least two of whom—he had it on high authority—were out-and-out spies. From there he launched into a pained recall of other incidents involving American and European agents who had tried—some with limited success—to pursue shameful careers of espionage in his own country.

It was not until he reached page eleven in his speech that Sobolev began to notice that the traffic of delegates padding out of the chamber was busier than usual. At page sixteen he became aware of one Far East delegation of five, plus five alternates, leaving in a body. Five pages later, as the sound of scraping chairs and swinging doors became more distracting, he looked up from his text to discover that he was speaking to an alarming number of vacant desks. Still he droned on. But the departures continued, and for those who remained it was amusing to watch the clumsy efforts of some to make their exits unobtrusive—on tiptoe and with nonchalant faces looking into space.

As he plodded into page twenty-nine, Sobolev came to a dead stop, scanned the chamber with a cold, piercing glint and addressed the chair.

"Mr. President," he said, switching into English and bristling with sarcasm, "may one inquire if a sudden epidemic of discomfort has taken our colleagues?"

Like the others who did not understand Russian, Sir Percy was wearing earphones used for speech translations. Tugging at the frame on his head, he said: "The chair does not understand the question. Does the Soviet delegate wish to continue his address?"

"Yes," Sobolev said. He leaned backward and whispered

to one of his alternates who nodded and walked briskly out of the chamber.

Sovolev read on for two more pages and stopped when his man hurried back to his side and whispered excitedly in his ear. A trembling wrath was on Sobolev's face when he looked up again and addressed the chair.

"Mr. President," he exclaimed, "I have never been insulted in my life as now! I have just been informed that the absent members of this chamber are in the lounge of the delegates—observing the match of baseball in Chicago on the television!"

Sir Percy looked strangely preoccupied, as if he had not heard Sobolev's outburst.

"Mr. President!" Sobolev roared. "I am addressing you!"

Sir Percy sat up with a start, as if from a doze, and as he leaned forward the wire leading to his earphones caught on the back of his chair, jerking the frame off his head. As it dropped, a tiny, white transistor radio no bigger than a cigarette lighter slipped out as if from his ear and clattered to his desk. The fall nudged the dial and suddenly the radio erupted with a bellow heard across the chamber—"*AND THE GAME IS OVER! ANOTHER THRILLER HERE AT COMISKEY PARK WHERE . . .*"

Flushed, his hands shaking, Sir Percy clicked off the sound and thrust the miniature set into his coat pocket. He uttered not a word; his embarrassment was total and devastating.

Sobolev's lips, flattened thin against his teeth, were almost white. "This is an affront," he said evenly, "that will not soon be forgotten." He turned toward the American delegation, shouting: "And perhaps we have Mr. Fulton to thank for the shameful spectacle of honorable"—he rolled the word around on his tongue—"delegates amusing themselves with observing baseball on the television when their duty is in this chamber!"

Fulton rose, rubbing a pencil on his chin. "I am sorry," he said, "if the delegate from the Soviet Union is shocked at members of this Assembly leaving the chamber. But was it not one of his countrymen who originated the United Nations walkout?"

Sobolev made no reply. He threw another glance at the empty desks, shuffled his papers and resumed his speech— to the new distraction of absent delegates returning from the lounge. As the speech drew near the end, Fulton folded a small piece of paper and sent it by page to Sir Percy. It read: *Please—the score.*

Sir Percy scribbled furtively on the note and sent it back. Fulton unfolded it slowly and read:

Dodgers 2
Sox 1

Eight hundred miles to the west, in the hotel suite that served as his Chicago office during the World Series, Commissioner Russell Kirk unfolded the yellow paper and read the message again:

THIS IS TO INFORM YOU THAT BY ORDER OF THE GOVERNMENT OF THE SOVIET UNION THE CHICAGO WHITE SOX ORGANIZATION IS FORBIDDEN BY THIS DIRECTIVE TO PARTICIPATE IN ANY FURTHER COMPETITIVE ACTIVITY UNTIL SUCH ACTION IS APPROVED BY MYSELF. SINCE THE FINAL MATCH OF THE TOURNAMENT IS SCHEDULED FOR TOMORROW IT IS EXPECTED THAT YOUR OFFICE WILL NOTIFY ALL INTERESTED PARTIES IMMEDIATELY THAT THIS ENGAGEMET IS NOW CANCELED UNTIL FURTHER NOTICE.

The telegram was signed: LEONID GALYNIN, AMBASSADOR, UNION OF SOVIET SOCIALIST REPUBLICS.

For the Commissioner, who was not known as a decisive man, this was the most shattering crisis of his life. His shirt was wrinkled from perspiration and the rim of his left ear was red and tender from almost three hours on the telephone.

Talking with Galynin in New York—he had finally traced him to Sobolev's apartment—had been fruitless. It made no difference to the Ambassador that the Sox and Dodgers were now tied at three games apiece and that the World

Series simply couldn't be held up at this stage. It would be held up, Galynin insisted, until the current dispute at the United Nations was settled. This decision would serve notice to the world, and especially to America, that the Communist bloc did not take lightly the outrageous insult to to Comrade Sobolev this afternoon and the Comrade Mendiata the day before yesterday. At the same time, it would dispel any doubt as to the Soviet Union's loyalty to its allies.

"But the weather's turning cold," Kirk groaned. "We've just got to get this last game played!"

Galynin's reply dripped acid. "Your baseball players wear one glove," he purred. "Let them wear another."

There were only two avenues for Kirk. He could postpone the final game, plead for the public's patience and pray that the debate would wind up in a day or two. And the wrath of the baseball world would fall on him. Or he could award the Series to the Dodgers by default. And the wrath of the baseball world would still fall on him.

So he had notified the interested parties—Bratton, Deborin, the Dodger management, the American League's Arnold Lang, the National League's Vernon Crowley, and directed his publicity department to release the awful news to the public. At any moment now the raucous bulletins would announce the indefinite postponement of the climax of the Series. And the nation would howl for his head.

The nation did—for his head, for Galynin's head, for Bukharov's head, for Mendiata's head, for Sobolev's head, for Fulton's head, for Sir Percy's head, and even for the heads of Bratton and Deborin and Crowley and Lang and anyone else who had had anything to do with the unbelievable mess. It did so in the streets and offices and stores and factories and beauty parlors and high schools and colleges and homes and mine shafts and planes and ships and at the tracking stations on the Dew Line. It did it on the sports page and the editorial page and on radio

and television. There were some who wanted to root out
Carlos Machado and his Cuban clan, wherever they were
holed up, and cast them out to sea. There were others who
were all for marching on the cemetery and toppling the
stone on the grave of Armistead E. Childers. It was a day
when boys cried and men cursed.

The following night, to make up for the unbearable baseball lull, the three television networks cleared their sched-
ules of all regular programing and pooled their resources
for a special documentary on the crisis, including portions
of the day's debate in the General Assembly. Bunny Beadle watched it with Tasia and her father in Tasia's suite
over a snack, and while it was an undeniably glum telecast
to look at, Beadle was concerned with the depth of Deborin's dejection. Except for a few half-hearted nibbles, the
Commissar, his eyes hollow and his manner listless, did not
touch his food, but sat slumped in his chair in utter silence.
Finally, during a film sequence of Kirk trying to explain
what had happened, Deborin rose and walked to the door
that separated his room and Tasia's. "I am tired," he said.
"I go to my room."

When the door closed, Beadle said to Tasia: "He's really
broken up over this, isn't he?"

"He has not talked much all day," Tasia said. "He is very
sad. He wishes to be alone."

The political part of the program was over, and now
there came a film of highlights of the World Series to date.
Beadle went to Deborin's door. "They're showing the hot
innings," he said, his voice raised. "How about it?"

"I do not wish to see it," Deborin's voice came through
the door. "I rest here, and think."

Beadle returned to the chair next to Tasia's. "Sometimes
he likes to stay at the window and look on the lake," she
said, "when he wishes to think to himself."

On the screen now they were in Boston again, and it
was the shouting, laughing moment of victory after the
winning of the pennant as the camera panned across the

locker room and showed the players throwing shoes and towels at each other and sipping champagne out of paper cups. Then Tasia giggled and Beadle frowned uncomfortably as the picture showed him displaying the ball with which he had made the last put-out that had cinched the flag. Then there was a closeup of his face, grotesque as he tried to grin with the huge lump of chewing tobacco in his right cheek, and Tasia laughed out loud as he pretended to hiss himself on the screen. The next scene showed Mike Dewar propelling her toward Beadle for the benefit of the photographers. "Look, me!" she squealed, "look, me!" It was the first time she had ever seen herself on television and the thrill of it made them forget, for the first time in many hours, the gloom that pressed on them. Then the tension went away and they laughed like children at Beadle's clumsy attempts to tuck in the loose flaps of his shirt as she stood by his side while the flash bulbs went off. And just as suddenly they were serious again, and silent, as they watched the photographer slip her arm into his.

The scene shifted to Comiskey Park and the start of the Series, but Beadle was no longer interested. "You know, Tasia," he said, his voice tender, "that's when I fell in love with you. That's exactly when it happened."

Tasia felt the warm glow spreading through her body. She knew, but with lovers it was a question that had to be asked. "When?" she said.

"That afternoon in Boston, when they put your arm in mine."

There was a trace of tease in Tasia's smile. "I should tell you," she said. "I helped a little."

"I'm glad you did, because you made it happen."

"I am glad too, Bunny."

"Tasia?"

"Yes?"

"Your arm—I want your arm in mine . . . for always."

Tasia slid off the chair and to her knees, beside Beadle. She touched his hands and stroked them. "My love, my love," she whispered, "this is what I want too . . . for always."

"Tasia, darling, I want you so much to marry me. I want you to belong to me, so much . . ."

He leaned to her and took her head in his hands and turned her face to his, and he saw a glisten in her eyes as if a tear had come and gone, and he kissed her.

He went to the television set and turned the knob and the picture disappeared into darkness, taking away the people who had been there, and with the figures on the screen went the rest of the world for now the world was just the two of them. They sat on the floor, hands clasped and offering whispers to each other, and smiles that said things only they could hear. But for all of the exquisite silence of their world, the whispers were loud in their hearts for they did not hear the door open on Deborin.

"We have been talking," Tasia said.

Deborin's shaggy eyebrows almost touched below his brow, and Beadle couldn't tell if he was angry or joshing. "I hope so," he said, watching them come to their feet.

But Tasia knew. "Father, you must not tease!" she exclaimed. "What has happened is very, very important. This is the most beautiful thing that has happened to me . . . Tonight, only now, Bunny has asked me that I marry him."

Bunny was so startled by her father's smile he started to say something—he didn't know what it would be—but found himself without words. Deborin ran his hand through hair that would never be tamed, and grinned. "I know that some day this will happen," he said. "I do not know that it will happen this night, but I am glad."

Tasia threw her arms around him. "Father, I am so happy!" she cried.

"It is this that is important," Deborin said, "that you are happy." He looked over her shoulder at Beadle. "That you will make her happy all of the life," he added.

"I love her very much, Mr. Deborin," Beadle said. "It's not often a man finds the perfect girl . . . I know I have."

"That is good, my boy," Deborin said. "Now I call you 'my boy'—is that not so?" He laughed, and winked at his daughter. "But you will not again call me the old Communist, no?"

Beadle was embarrassed as Deborin went on: "No, you must not again call me the old Communist. This makes me much angry—because, you see, I am not old!"

Beadle smiled nervously. "That was a while back," he said. "Love changes things."

A shade of melancholy returned to Deborin's face. "Yes, love it changes things," he said, as though talking to himself. "Is it not sad that there is love in peoples, and the world is peoples, but there is not love in the world. . . ."

Tasia moved nearer to Beadle and took his hand. Deborin crossed his arms over his chest and spread out his feet. "I am happy, my boy," he said. "I am happy for Tasia, and I am happy for you. This is a much, much big decision you make tonight."

"I couldn't be surer of anything, Mr. Deborin," Beadle said, pleased but still puzzled that the Commissar's mood had changed so swiftly.

Deborin paced the length of the room and back. The quick step of old was in his legs again, and now there was life in his eyes. He started to take another stride then whirled around, fingers stroking the dip of his hawky nose. He gave Beadle a stern, businesslike stare. "I also have make a much big decision," he said. "We play!"

Beadle looked at him blankly. He was bewildered.

"We play!" Deborin repeated. "We play the baseball, you do not understand? I think and I think, and I make the decision. We finish the tournament of the World Series —on the day after tomorrow!"

Beadle almost shouted as he drew Tasia to him and hugged her waist. "This is terrific!" he exclaimed. "You're going to fight Galynin? And Bukharov?"

"I fight nobody," Deborin said soberly. "I am the chairman of the Chicago White Sox. The order of the Ambassador it is to me not correct. It is not justice. I do not disobey my government, but I disobey the man who does a thing that is not justice. Some things a man must do when he thinks in him it is correct. This, now, I do!"

Beadle, his arm still around Tasia's waist, whirled her about the room in a half-dance.

Deborin looked at his watch. "This is not the time to jump and to dance," he said. "We have much things to do, and the time it advances quickly. We must tell Bratton, and the Commissioner, and the others. Quickly! You talk in this telephone, I talk in my telephone." He broke into a jog toward his room, then stopped at the door and looked at the two of them in the center of the room. "The day after tomorow," he said, winking again. "After the match— then it will be the time to jump and dance."

14

It was a game that Horace Bratton would remember all of his life and, quite possibly, wherever he went in the hereafter. The fact that one of the teams was playing in defiance of the owners was only one of its unique aspects.

The final contest of this World Series was destined to become part of history as the first—and likely the last—to be played to a standing-room-only crowd in the street. Even though the absolute impossibility of securing a single ticket under any condition had been publicized over and over in the press and on the air, an astonishing two thousand don't-care hopefuls showed up at the main gate anyway, ready to meet the outrageous ransom demands of scalpers. But the scalpers, who knew a hopeless situation when unusual events set one up, had stayed home like any other sane no-ticket citizen to watch the game on television. What was remarkable about the overflow of fans was that most of them had come to Comiskey Park prepared to stay the afternoon on the outside. They were equipped with portable radios, folding chairs, sandwiches, coffee-gurgling Thermoses and a determination—made clear to the stunned police detail—to "be" at the game even if they couldn't get inside the park. They wanted at least the nearness and the sound and the smell of the frenzy inside, and many of them were there on the chance that they might see—and perhaps touch—Mikhail Deborin, the man who dared flout his Communist bosses. Since they would not be denied, the police had roped off the intersection fronting the gates and detoured it to traffic. And there they stood and sat, shivering and stomping their feet for warmth— ears bent to the radio, eyes wistfully on the high walls before them.

An unnerved policeman turned up his collar against the raw wind. "I don't believe it," he said to his sergeant. "I see it, but I don't believe it."

For the crowd within, quivering from the cold and with the rapture of the moment, the unbelievable came early in the game when Sox catcher Lee Sanford, the team's notoriously weak hitter, connected with a homerun—first of his Major League career—giving Chicago a one-run lead in the second inning. When Sanford trudged back to the dugout he was so aghast at what he had done that trainer Nick Dorsey had to practically pour a cup of black coffee down his throat to tranquilize him. But when the Dodgers came up for their third at bat, starter Jenk Simms pitched into trouble again—the Dodgers reaching third and first on a walk, a wild pitch and a single.

Bratton tugged at the zipper on his windbreaker and gave it an angry jerk. "There he goes, losing his control again," he said. "What bugs me is we could've wrapped this up with Reeves here!"

He turned to Deborin, huddled in silence beside him. "I think I'll yank him," he said.

"Give to him time," Deborin cautioned. "The day it is cold, and he is not already warm."

Simms executed a strikeout but the next batter stroked a long sacrifice fly, tying the score. When Simms followed this with three straight balls to the next batter, Deborin mounted the dugout steps. "I call a moratorium," he said to Bratton over his shoulder, "and go to talk to him."

As Deborin began his rapid stride to the mound, there erupted from almost fifty-two thousand throats a low, discordant hubbub of howls and roars and what sounded like wild yelps of laughter. Here, at last, was the man of the hour emerging into view for the first time in the game, and the figure he cut on the field brought the multitude to its feet. That morning, as he paced his hotel room waiting to embark on the collision course he had deliberately charted, Deborin had listened to the forecasts of wintry weather, and now he was prepared for the cold. Dangling almost to his ankles was the long, black overcoat that Nadezhda had bought him that last winter in Kiev, the seal collar framing his shoulders, and on his head perched a jaunty karakul, the whole giving him the air of a dismounted Cossack reporting to the Czar. By the time he got to Simms, the clamor had turned into a crescendo of cheers and even the bloc of California fans near the visitors' dugout was clapping ardently.

There was a warm hand, too, for Simms when he got out of the inning with no further damage but it subsided immediately when the voice on the public address system crackled:

"Attention, please. Your attention, please! Here is a bulletin from New York . . . 'The General Assembly of the United Nations this afternoon declined, by a two-thirds majority, to adjudicate the Cuban-American crisis and directed the state departments of the two countries to arbitrate the dispute among themselves' . . . I repeat: 'The General Assembly—' "

The rest was drowned out in a massive squall of jubilation that thundered through the park for a full minute. Bratton and the players looked at Deborin, but his face showed no emotion. Instead, he turned to Simms and said, in a low voice: "A day like now, it is difficult for the arm and for the heart. I tell to you this—put your thought to Jim Reeves in the hospital, and it will be good again."

The unbelievable continued. In the fifth inning, with not even a fleck of sleet to give warning, a light snow began to fall. It sent a shudder through the stands but the crowd quickly shrugged it off when the Sox broke out with back-to-back singles followed by a Dodger bobble of an easy fly in the slippery outfield, forging ahead again two to one.

In the sixth inning Deborin smiled for the first time that day. "Now things are good to us," he told Bratton. "Now I have the taste—how do you say?—at the mouth."

"Me too," Bratton said. "Keep your fingers crossed and maybe—"

The trainer was tugging at Deborin's coat. "You're wanted in the clubhouse," he said. "Long distance."

Deborin was on the phone through the seventh inning and part of the eighth, and on his return to the dugout the blaring radio and the mighty echoes from outside told him the Dodgers had taken a three-two lead. Bratton saw the glum, pensive look on his face, and he masked his own dejection. "We'll get those runs back," he said. "Lots of time."

The Commissar was struggling into the overcoat he had removed in the clubhouse. "For you, yes," he said. "For me, no."

"What d'you mean?" Bratton said. "Who was that?" He threw up his hands before Deborin could speak. "Never mind," he said. "I know. Anybody calling you here at the park, it's got to be Bukharov."

"It is Ambassador Galynin who calls, in New York."

"Oh, Lord, what did he want?"

"This time, at last, he wants nothing," Deborin sighed. He motioned for Bratton to follow him to an empty spot at the end of the bench where they would be alone. "For you it is, I think, a rejoice," he said, his voice low. "My government, it has just make the decree. It no more wishes the property of the organization of the Chicago White Sox. Galynin, he tells to me that Moscow tells to him that we abandon everything."

Bratton's mouth dropped. He heard the crack of a hit but it seemed something remote, not now a part of him, and he didn't even turn to look at the field. "What d'you know!" was all he could say. "Well, what d'you know!"

Deborin wrapped his fingers around a button on his coat and twirled it aimlessly. "The superiors of Galynin," he said, "they tell to him the experiment it is a . . . a much bad failure. Now it is finish."

"My God! What happens now?"

"For me, I do not know, but I will know early. My government, it has decide to sell the organization to a buyer in America—I do not know who. Galynin and Bukharov, now they fly to Chicago and they wish a meeting of emergency tomorrow at the hour of noon."

"So quick?"

"Yes. All who take part before in the things of the estate of Mr. Childers, they must come at the meeting. You, also."

"I'll be there. My God, this is fantastic!"

"Fastic?"

"It shakes a guy up. What's going to happen?"

Deborin rose and looked out of the dugout, scanning the snowy sky. Flakes fell on his arm and he watched their melting twinkle until they were gone. "I know only," he said softly, "what this is to me. I have lost my club."

For a long moment he seemed lost in reverie, but as the team hustled into the dugout from the field he slapped his hands together and suddenly the zest of earlier innings was back. "Later we talk about this, Horace," he said. "But now the engagement, yes?"

In their box on the third-base line, Tasia and Miss Wiley huddled together for warmth. "Poor Bunny," Tasia said, shouting above the chorus of bellows around her. "I think he is cold."

Miss Wiley was cheerful. "He comes up to bat this time," she chirped. "He'll get a hit and somebody'll knock him in. You just watch!"

But Beadle did not get a hit. He and Sanford and Nelson went down in order.

The mass hoarseness in the stands and the rumble of stomping feet were like a continuous series of detonations, each one muffling the one before, as the throngs sensed the approach of a climax. And still the snow fell.

Now it was the last chance for the White Sox—their final turn at bat in the ninth, with two out and Ken Powers on second base. To Bratton, it seemed that Powers had been there a very long time, and as he rummaged his mind for the odds, he knew full well that they had all gone but one. In millions of homes the announcer was uttering the ritual commom to such situations . . . "and now it's up to Sal Castinez to keep this game alive . . ."

As Salvatore Castinez rose off his knee in the batter's circle, Deborin bounded up the dugout steps. "I think of something," he shouted to Bratton. He got his time out and as the stands rocked with rhythmic hand-clapping, he looked into the mulatto face of the somber Puerto Rican.

"Salvatore," he said, "you remember long before, one day, you make the—the cross on you when you arrive at the plate to bat, and I become much angry at you?"

Castinez showed a glisten of white teeth. "Yeah," he smiled, "I remember."

Deborin looked at the ground, shuffling his feet. He seemed to be groping for words. "I command you, that day, never to again do that," he said, finally.

"I never done it, Mr. Deborin," Castinez said.

"I know. But now, I permit you, if you wish, to make the cross on the body."

Castinez smiled again. "Now it's okay?"

Deborin's thick eyebrows furrowed. "Yes," he said, "but you understand I permit this only because you think it is a thing of good luck to you. I think it make you feel much good, so I permit."

Castinez lifted a heel and tapped a blob of mud off his spikes. "Thanks, Mr. Deborin," he said.

Umpire Len Hilts was walking toward them, tugging impatiently at his chest protector. Deborin leaned closer to Castinez and put his hand on his arm. "I tell to you one more thing only," he said in a loud whisper while a shy, boyish grin swept away the lines of weariness on his face.

"I will be much happy if you do not tell to anyone this. It will be good if it is the secret of you only, and me only."

Castinez nodded. Only a very keen observer would have noticed the gesture that followed.

At the plate, Castinez fixed his eyes on the pitcher, the bat motionless behind him. He looked at two pitches that were tempting but just barely off the strike zone, and fouled one to the left of third base. The next ball curved in low and inside, the kind of pitch that was to Castinez like a gopher to a hawk. He swooped hungrily, his massive shoulders making an almost audible wrench.

For an agonizing moment the ball was lost in the snow's white haze, then it reappeared again in a swift fall directly into the railing of the left-field bleachers and the repressed, screaming hordes, now unquestionably gone mad, let go with a monumental roar.

Still there was to be one last instance of the unbelievable.

Castinez ran like a panicked antelope, with such gigantic strides that when Powers was approaching third base he was but a few paces behind his teammate. His head down as he galloped, the din making a music of ecstasy in his soul, he did not see Powers slip on the patch of snow as he rounded third and, knees suddenly buckling, sink grotesquely to the ground. Nor could he hear the snap of Powers' ankle just before he dropped. It was only when Powers, his face an ugly contortion of pain, tried to rise and slid again to his knees that the harrowing whimper of the crowd brought Castinez to a sudden halt about six feet short of the prostrate form off the third-base line. Castinez stared at Powers who was moaning "I can't! I can't!" and now the commotion in the stands stopped and a hush fell on the park as every man on the field—including the Sox who had scrambled out of the dugout—stood motionless like snow-specked statues. The eerie silence, the awful stillness were but a moment, though they could have been an eternity. Suddenly the long-coated figure of Mikhail Deborin broke from the group at the dugout and rushed forward.

"Pick him up!" Deborin yelled. "Pick him up and carry him home!"

Castinez, eyes glazed, glanced blankly at Deborin and at Powers on the ground. Umpire Hilts, the enormity of it all finally pricking him to life, bounded toward the outlandish scene.

"In your arms take him!" Deborin shouted. "Carry him home!"

At this, Bratton came running, waving his arms and screaming "No! No!" but it was too late. Castinez, his mind as if a blur, ran toward Powers and slipping and struggling in the ooze, gathered him up in one mighty lunge and, holding him as if cradling a baby, trotted home and deposited him gently—bottom first—on the plate. Then with Powers blinking at him in disbelief, Castinez thrust out his right foot like a ballerina starting an arabesque and tapped the vertex with the toe of his spikes.

Had there been a dome atop Comiskey Park the cataclysm would have made it a volcano, the lava of delirious rapture sprewing over the city.

On the field, it was quite another matter—a scene that no two persons who were there that memorable afternoon would recall exactly alike.

Hilts, who was heading for the accident near third, had reversed himself when Castinez picked up the crippled Powers and, his soggy belly-pad bobbing like a piston, had cantered after the absurd-looking pair until they reached the plate. There he did an amazing thing: he arched his arm, pointed thumb quivering, in possibly the most eloquent out sign he had ever executed. Then panic seized him and he looked from Castinez to Powers and back at Castinez again, as if wondering which of the two he had called out—or was it both?—and his head went into a spastic shake, for this simply had to be a nightmare. And then, his brain seemingly cleared as the preposterous sight disentangled itself at the plate, he spread out his hands, palms down, and bellowed: *"SAFE!"*

The pantomime was barely over when the opposing brains trusts came hurtling at him from both dugouts—crusty Dodger manager Stogie Curtle and his coaches, Bratton and Deborin and their coaches, and every man in uniform including the two batboys. For a shrieking, ranting four minutes Hilts found himself jutting chins with Curtle then Bratton then Curtle then Bratton again, until the three base umpires pulled him bodily out of the morass of waving arms, howls of frustration, shaking fists and a litany of coarse suggestions about his eyesight, his intellect, his ancestry and his patriotism—including a shriek from Dodger pinch-hitter Red Durham that he was a Communist. The four umpires retired to the now empty infield for an official conference, but the anguished yelps of Curtle and Bratton and the others followed them there.

What did he mean—safe? Who ever heard of a player being carried to the plate?

What did he mean—out? Powers had done nothing wrong and the rule book said he couldn't be denied his run!

But the rule book said the runner must reach home under his own power!

Oh yeah? What about the act-of-God situation?

Ridiculous! Castinez had touched a teammate while both were running the bases!

So what! There was no rule said a runner's out if he touches another runner!

Well, why didn't the Sox send in a pinch-runner, for God's sakes?

Because the umpire didn't call time, meathead!

You don't call time after a homerun, birdbrain! A homer's an automatic time out!

And so the rhubarb went on the field, its sparks igniting brush fires of argument in the stands, some of them fanning into fist fights.

At last the umpires' conference broke up, and Hilts ordered Bratton and Curtle to clear the field immediately of all players. The three other umpires walked in silence to the first-base area and stood there, not a face betraying the verdict. Hilts, Bratton, Deborin, and Curtle stood in a semicircle on the pitcher's mound. Now only a strange, almost mournful murmur rustled through the stands. The nation waited.

Hilts slipped off his protector and dropped it on the ground. He eyed the three men coldly.

"First of all," he said in clipped tones, "I'm not going to apologize for that double call. There's just no precedent for what's happened here—nothing, nothing at all to go by.

"Now, because of the way this—this cockeyed thing got started, and because of the way we're calling it, and all this goof-off with no rule about a guy carrying another guy, we decided we got to announce the call, and tell why and everything, on the public address system. Or there's going to be a riot here in two minutes. I'll announce it. And this is what it is:

"In a thing, in an accident like this, there's nothing says a runner's out if he touches another runner. What's more, there's nothing says a runner can't carry another runner. So he's safe on that—"

Bratton grabbed at Deborin's arm. "We made it!" he blurted, trying to keep his voice down.

Hilts glared at them, nettled by the interruption.

"But what most everybody missed," he went on, "and I did myself for a minute, is that Castinez overran the runner. So we're calling it an out for ——"

Bratton threw up his one arm and shook his fist. "He did not pass him!" he roared.

"He did!" Curtle roared back. "He did!"

Hilts' tone was unruffled. "Castinez passed him between third and home," he said, "when he went round in front of Powers to pick him up. No more than a foot or two, maybe, but he passed him. For that—he's out."

Bratton raised his eyes to the heavens and slapped

himself on the brow. "But he didn't pass him, Len!" he shouted. "He didn't!"

Deborin put his hand on Bratton's arm. "The arbitrator is correct," he said in a gentle voice. "I observe the foot of Castinez in front of Powers."

Hilts looked at Bratton, and a flash of compassion showed in his eyes. "Sorry, Horace," he said. "It's all over."

Deborin looked away from the group, away from the mass of faces in the stands, beyond the high walls of the park and into the bleak clouds at the nearness of the womb of winter. Into his thoughts raced the fluctuations of fate that had so swiftly taken from him first the daughter he cherished, then the club he had come to love, and now the triumph he had wanted so badly to quell his scandalous disobedience to Moscow on foreign soil. He was hurt, now, deaf to the thousands chanting his name as they awaited the verdict, and the loneliness closed in on him again.

In the conference room of the late Armistead E. Childers, the Communist dignitaries, austere and thorough as always, had conducted the meeting with their usual brevity. But in half an hour they had said a great deal, for Miss Wiley's brand-new note pad was already half-filled with the hurried strokes of her shorthand. Ambassador Galynin, speaking directly to Bradley and Daniels (as if purposely snubbing Deborin and Bratton who sat on the same side of the long table), had come immediately to the point: while the Soviet Union still appreciated and admired Mr. Childers' inspiring gesture of goodwill, the whole matter of the estate had been an interesting experiment but, sad to say, it had failed. It had brought about too many distractions, and created too much discord to justify its continuance. Now it was ended, and the Ambassador hoped that the final disposal of the estate would be satisfactory to all concerned. Galynin was followed by Valentin Kononov, the trade attaché, who conveyed his government's instructions that the twenty hotels which had been converted to employee ownership remain as such, except that henceforth they would be operated under the trusteeship of the United States government. Similarly, the Soviet Union had already begun proceedings to relinquish the Chicago Belye Chulki, a report on which would be made by Comrade Bukharov. It was his government's sincere hope, Kononov emphasized, that this development would tame the American government's aggressive, stubborn stand in the Cuban crisis and speed the surrender of that country's defectors.

Bukharov, who had been whispering to Fedor Malsynenko, the melancholy *Pravda* correspondent, rose to his turn. In regard to the disposal of the baseball team, he said, he and his comrades here present had agreed that what the Americans called "first refusal rights" on the purchase should be granted to Mr. Jack Huggins, former president of Horizon Enterprises, original owner of the Belye Chulki who had sold the club to Mr. Childers. Indeed, Bukharov crowed, he had last night and again this morning been in contact with Mr. Huggins who was most interested in repossessing the club, and it was expected that the sale would be consummated within the week.

Commissioner Kirk and American League president Arnold Lang, admitted to the meeting as official observers, nodded approvingly. Bukharov removed his thick glasses and turned his plump figure toward Deborin.

"And now," he said, a sneer twitching at his mouth, "we are at the end of this strange episode. The services of Commissar Deborin, all will understand, are no longer needed in this country. It is the expectation of my government that Commissar Deborin will make preparations immediately to depart for his homeland in the time of three days, accompanied"—he threw Malsynenko a knowing glance—"by his daughter."

Bukharov looked around the table and replaced his glasses. "That is all," he said. Then he sat down.

Deborin placed his hands on the table and pushed himself up. "I beg the pardon," he said, his voice firm and resonant. "That is not all."

He made a futile swipe at his hair and looked at the Russians across the table. "All last night I have not the sleep," he said. "At the window in my room I stand, and I think much. I think of something I think of much before —many weeks. And I have make the decision . . . I stay. I stay here, in the United States of America."

In the hush that followed, Miss Wiley's ball-point pen dropping to the carpet made a jarring sound. Deborin took a deep breath and went on:

"For this thing I do, there are three reasons. By the players of baseball, which I have been with so much, I have learn much about the people here, and the way of life here. What I have learn, I have like. I much hope, also, that by me and what I have said and did in this country as chairman of the club there happens—how do you say? —the vice versa. I hope the American peoples have learn some things about the Russian peoples they do not know before."

Deborin's hand absently touched Lang's ashtray and moved it back and forth. "Second, my daughter Tasia and Bunny Beadle, which now wait for me in the office that adjoins, will marry to each other. So I report to Mr. Bukharov that my daughter she has not any plans to return to the Soviet Union."

Bukharov blanched, and Galynin through his pince-nez gave him such a withering look that Malsynenko charitably turned his head away.

Now a faint smile came to Deborin's face, and for the first time since yesterday's heartbreak his eyes danced. "And last," he said, "the result of the tournament of World Series it make me what the Americans call . . . a loser. To everybody it is known what happens, in my country, to losers . . . soon they are in Siberia."

The Commissar sat down, still smiling, and said: "I do not like, in Siberia, the climate."

The pock-marks on Galynin's face seemed to have turned pink. "I have nothing to say on this matter here," he snapped. "The meeting is concluded. Gentlemen, we leave."

Malsynenko bounded ahead and opened the door for the Ambassador who marched through, staring straight ahead. Behind Galynin strode Kononov, with Bukharov bringing up the rear. Suddenly, as the others at the table stared in silence, Miss Wiley scurried to the wall behind her, gathered up the Russian flag that Bukharov had left behind months before, and swept off after him. "Here," she said, "take this with you."

"Foolish woman!" Bukharov snarled, snatching it from her hands. But there was one final ignominy in store for him. As he plodded forward, flag in hand, to catch up with the others, he forgot to lower the staff and it struck the upper ledge of the doorway and snapped back, the metal bulb rapping him sharply on the head and knocking off his glasses. "Foolish woman!" he repeated, pulling himself together. Then he stomped out.

Bradley and Daniels shook hands all around and hurried off to Daniels' office. Kirk and Lang said their goodbys and hurried off to keep a pledge to meet the press in the reception room. Deborin and Bratton followed Miss Wiley into her office to join Tasia and Beadle.

Deborin put his hands around his daughter. "It is done," he said.

"Father!" Tasia exclaimed. "Now you will be here for my marrying, and you will give me to Bunny!"

Beadle stood by, grinning. "You look just like that day you came off the plane," he said.

"That was a good day," Deborin sighed. "Today, also, is a good day."

Bratton moved forward, his empty sleeve slapping against his jacket. "One thing I'm telling you, Mike," he said. "When Huggins gets the team again, he gets you and me to manage—not just me. That's a promise."

Deborin laughed. "We talk later about this," he said. "But it is nice."

Beadle took Tasia's hand. "We're taking you all to lunch," he said.

Deborin looked at Bratton. "Horace, you go with the young ones," he said. "Me, I wish just a cup of tea, and Miss Wiley—this she make with excellence." He flashed a saucy smile at her. "You have for me some tea?" he said.

"Dear me," Miss Wiley stammered, "of course. Right away!" And when she reached for the kettle, she noticed that her finger tips were rubbing together again.